"I really did scare you, didn't I?"

Edgar asked, wrapping an arm around her. "Your heart is beating like crazy."

Dee pushed herself away from him as she inhaled the scent of his spicy aftershave. "I've just been..." She couldn't tell him she'd been reading about him. Let alone daydreaming about working together.

"You were just what?" He studied her intently. "Are you sure you're okay, Dee?"

She tried to shake it off. Between the phone call she'd received and feeling that someone had followed her into the library...and thinking about Edgar, there were plenty of things to be shaken up about.

* * *

REUNION REVELATIONS: Secrets surface when old friends—and foes—get together.

Books by Carol Steward

Love Inspired Suspense

Guardian of Justice #83
In His Sights #96

In the Line of Fire

Love Inspired

There Comes a Season #27
Her Kind of Hero #56
Second Time Around #92
Courting Katarina #134
This Time Forever #165
Finding Amy #263
Finding Her Home #282
Journey to Forever #301

CAROL STEWARD

To Carol Steward, selling a book is much like riding a roller coaster—every step of the process, every sale brings that exhilarating high. During the less exciting times, she's busy gathering ideas and refilling her cup. Writing brings a much-needed balance to her life, as she has her characters share lessons she has learned, as well.

When she's not working at the University of Northern Colorado, you can usually find her spending time with her husband of over thirty years, writing and thanking God she survived raising her own three children to reap His rewards of playing with her adorable grandchildren.

Throughout all the different seasons of life, God has continued to teach Carol to turn to Him. She has also learned to simplify her life and appreciate her many blessings—His gift of creativity, sharing her love for God with readers and setting an example of what God can do when we say, "Yes, God, take me, shape me, use me." To find out more about Carol's slightly crazy life and her books, visit her Web site at www.carolsteward.com.

In His Sights

CAROL STEWARD

Steeple
Hill®

Published by Steeple Hill Books™

Special thanks and acknowledgment are given to Carol Steward for her contribution to the REUNION REVELATIONS miniseries.

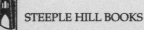

STEEPLE HILL BOOKS

Steeple
Hill®

ISBN-13: 978-0-373-44286-7
ISBN-10:   0-373-44286-6

IN HIS SIGHTS

www.SteepleHill.com

Printed in U.S.A.

Jesus said, "I have told you these things, so that in me you may have peace. In this world you will have trouble. But take heart! I have overcome the world."
—*John* 16:33

To Val, Shirlee, Margaret, Lenora and Marty,
my coconspirators—my light in the shadows.
You're the greatest!

ONE

Something had to be wrong. The caller ID showed her sister's number, and Lauren knew not to call her at work.

"Deandra Owens, how may I help you?" she answered out of habit. "Sorry, Lauren. What's up?"

"It's happening again, Dee. There's another warning on the Web site."

Dee hadn't heard Lauren this frantic in weeks.

"Log on the site, now," her sister demanded. "Hurry!"

Dee swung her chair to the computer and moved her mouse to pull up the site. "Magnolia Falls: Where Are They Now?" scrolled to the top of the computer monitor and the photograph from the reunion began to load. "Where?"

"Someone put a picture of the group at the reunion on there," Lauren said.

"I did," Dee said with a sigh of relief.

"Yes, on the home page, but, it's in the blog now—with flames burning over it."

"You *can't* be serious!" Her mind raced to the angry posts they'd received in the guest book. Dee stared as the blog loaded, her pulse racing. She scrolled through the comments, then came to the digitally altered photo posted by Anonymous and gasped. "Who would do this?"

"The police never even figured out who sent that entry last month."

Dee looked for some clue, ignoring her sister.

"The one telling us that someone on campus isn't who they seem to be."

"Yes, I remember," Dee said. "I'm—"

The fear in Lauren's voice returned. "We have to do something."

The police hadn't given the Web site much attention, claiming pranks and inappropriate postings were pretty common on any public site. Dee stared at the photo in disbelief. Who would have such anger toward those at the reunion?

"Dee…"

"Where are you, Lauren?"

"I'm at Seth's with Jake. Seth has a late appointment today."

Lauren had had enough scares in the recent months. Dee didn't want to see it start all over again. "Stay put and lock the doors." Dee looked up to see, Edgar Ortiz, the assistant director of admissions in her doorway, pointing at his watch. "Thanks for calling. I'll call you back after the press conference."

"Dee, you ready?" The handsome Brazilian made her heart flutter, even when she wasn't under stress.

"Just a minute, Edgar. I need to fix a little problem right away." Her hands were shaking.

He stepped to her side. "Can I help?"

"No, thanks, it'll just take a minute."

"We're in a hurry. The police need a minute to prep you." He leaned closer, making her nerves that much worse.

"I'll be right there, just hold them off for a minute. You know, work your charm."

He cleared his throat and headed for the door. "You're the charmer. That is why we hired you."

Dee highlighted the name of the picture and all of the Java script that went with it, then read the options she had for removing the data from the blog: "Remove Locally" or "Remove locally and from server." She tried to reason out which would keep it so the police could trace it. One option would keep it on her computer, but remove it from the site. The other would remove it from everywhere. Dee moved the mouse to "Remove Locally" and thought it through again before clicking the button.

"Dee, come on." Edgar paused as he stepped through the door, his voice full of annoyance.

She jumped and with one slip of the wrist, she hit the wrong button and everything was gone.

Edgar leveled her a stare and she felt the emptiness in the pit of her stomach. Temporary or not, every day they were together they always seemed to be needling each other.

She picked up her notes and rushed out the door after him. "Someone's posting harassing messages on the Web site again, and thanks to you, I just lost the evidence."

"Yes, I saw the flaming picture. I was going to talk to you about it *after* the press conference. Maybe it's time you just give up on the Web site." He waited for her to walk beside him, then pushed a stray hair from her face.

How could he be so cavalier about it? "You're one of the people in the picture, Edgar. We don't know who they're targeting." She never went into a press conference so distracted.

"Miss Owens, we need you to read this release also," Detective Jim Anderson said as he handed her a sheet of paper.

Dee read it, then glanced through the doorway to the members of the press watching her every reaction. "In here please." She walked into the empty office and turned to Detective Anderson. "You've had this information for weeks, since Cassie Winters planted the memorial garden. Why haven't you said something sooner?"

"We've run out of leads with what we had. We're hoping that we can flush out the person if he or she thinks we have more information to go on," the detective responded.

Dee struggled to regain her composure as she

watched Edgar walk to the back of the room with the other college administrators.

She loved Magnolia College. She had to make that come across, above all else.

Look pleasant.

Professional. She forced a smile and realized it was overdone. She couldn't look happy, sharing terrible news like this.

She didn't want to look disrespectful.

She took a deep breath to steady herself before facing the cameras. With a serious smile on her face, she gazed past the reporters and cameras to Edgar.

This was about the college they both loved.

People they cared about.

Edgar had been dead set on getting her position as a PR specialist soon after the construction crew had uncovered a woman's skeleton on campus. Yet in less than six months, they'd had three huge scandals that rocked the community's foundation, and would likely hurt enrollment if they didn't do some damage control immediately. Edgar—and his boss—weren't happy with the rash of negative publicity. That was perfectly clear.

"The faculty and staff at Magnolia College are shocked by recent events involving our tight-knit community." She took a quick breath for strength. "We are deeply saddened by the shooting of three individuals with ties to Magnolia College. The three were following leads in the death of talented alumnus, Scott Winters. Scott graduated two-and-a-half years ago with his bachelor's degree in Journalism and went on to write for the *Savannah Herald*. The victims are identified as Scott's sister, Cassie Winters, Professor Jameson King, and former teammate of Scott's, Kevin Reed. All three have been treated and released from the hospital.

"The police have made two arrests in connection with the shootings, which took place at the old sugar mill in Riverton. Both are being held in the city jail and will undergo questioning in relation to an alleged point-shaving scheme, as well as the murder of Scott Winters."

Dee paused, waiting for the lump in her throat to dissipate. She fought to get the image of Scott's sister out of her head. *I can't think of Cassie or I'll never get through this.*

Dee could see the administrators cringe, those whose faces didn't look like they were carved from stone. Her stomach churned. "The Magnolia Falls Police Department expect to reveal at least one more suspect soon." Hands immediately raised, but Dee knew what they wanted. "I'm sorry, we will not be revealing the suspects' names at this time."

She pulled out the prepared statement given to her by the police chief and noticed her hands shaking. She took a deep breath. "The staff at Magnolia College is cooperating fully with authorities. We ask the public to respect the school's responsibility to protect the privacy of every member of our staff and student population. Progress is being made on both the recovered skeleton and the point-shaving cases, but we would like to remind the community that these *are* ongoing investigations, and the details must be kept confidential in order not to compromise the integrity of the investigations."

Dee cleared her throat and took a sip of water. "The police chief has asked me to update the public on evidence found in relation to the unidentified woman's skeleton. A charm, found during the planting of the Scott Winters Memorial Garden, is now believed to be key evidence. Crime-scene investigators have determined a set of initials on the charm and believe it will open up new leads. If you have information related to any of these cases, you are asked to contact the Magnolia Falls Police Department directly.

"Magnolia College will continue to provide our students with an excellent education and will maintain a normal schedule. Thank you."

Television stations from all over the region had come to cover these events, and the room was filled to capacity. Dee shifted behind the podium and pointed to a reporter who refused to be ignored.

The young man looked to be about Scott Winters's age. "Miss Owens, what is being done to ensure student safety?"

"I will point out that Magnolia College has the second lowest crime rate in the region. We have not seen any increase in crime on campus since the skeleton was found. However, we are taking every precaution possible. In addition to seminars on personal safety, new emergency phones have been installed along the inner-campus walkways, and patrols have increased. The college did go through a major security upgrade just two years ago."

She glanced to the back of the room and saw Edgar leaving before the press conference was finished. While she couldn't help but feel she'd let him down, she was also furious. He'd touted her as the "Queen of Spin" when it came to recovering from bad publicity. But what did he expect after a second murder connected to Magnolia College?

Dee regained her composure and continued. "The upgrade included key cards for external entrances to every dorm and building holding evening classes. Security cameras are in place in many undisclosed locations. The college is in the top ten on safety studies. The board of trustees is gathering information on whether further changes need to be made."

Hands shot up, and Dee nodded to another reporter. "I've heard rumors that some Magnolia College staff are involved in the point-shaving scheme. Are they going to be fired?" she asked.

Another reporter stood up. "What about the coaching staff? To what extent is Coach Nelson involved?"

Dee held up one hand until the room quieted, regaining control. "One question at a time, please. Chairman J. T. Kessler has called for a special session of the board of trustees this week to discuss possible disciplinary action for any involved faculty and coaching personnel. Until then, no further details will be released."

As she answered each question, her mind drifted back to Edgar. Though he had been forced to reduce their recruitment team, the two of them were working hard. She had thought they were becoming close, and she realized, with disappointment, how much his approval meant to her.

What more did he expect of her?

TWO

"I told you to stop calling. In case you missed it, I have enough problems without…" The deep voice growled.

"And I thought you were going to scare Dee Owens off. We can't have her sticking her nose into the investigation!"

"You're getting paranoid…"

"Well, now, that's like the pot calling the kettle black, isn't it?" There was an awkward silence, filled with tension as one waited for the other to continue. "I need more money. If you aren't going to get rid of Dee, I'll have to find someone else to do it."

"Dee Owens doesn't know anything more than what the cops tell her. Quit worrying. I'm keeping tabs on her—and that ridiculous Web site. Just lay low! Stop sending e-mails. If I were you, I'd get out of the country while you can."

"I would if I could, believe me. If I could count on

you to clean up this mess once and for all, that is. Dee may not know anything *yet*. All she needs is another chance to dig deeper. Get rid of her. Now!"

THREE

Dee and her friend Steff Kessler, director of alumni relations, spent the afternoon brainstorming ideas to counteract the scandals. They figured out a way to pull a list of distinguished alumni from the college database and they drafted a letter requesting alumni get involved. Dee hadn't been this encouraged in weeks. Excited to move forward with the campaign as soon as possible, she left a message for Edgar.

She tidied her desk after Steff headed back to her office in the library. Dee reviewed her notes, jotting additional suggestions in the margins as she waited for Edgar to return her call. At a little after five o'clock, she decided Edgar wasn't going to call. Dee placed the drafted letter into her briefcase.

As soon as Dee closed her office door the phone rang. She hurried back inside, dropped the purse back into the chair and lifted the receiver, hoping it was Edgar returning her call. "Deandra Owens, how can I—"

The caller interrupted Dee. Static mingled with

hushed words. "Miss Owens, you must help—" the woman said before her Southern accented voice cut out.

"What?" Dee waited a few seconds then tried to get the caller's attention. "Hello?"

"Those...on the reunion Web site—" The caller was interrupted by yelling and commotion on her end.

Dee could hear doors slamming, then more static. "Hello?" She considered hanging up but couldn't. Two words had her hooked—Web site. How could anyone know she'd just taken over as Webmaster? "Hello, are you there?" She looked down at the caller ID, which read "unknown number."

"Just a moment, please," the caller whispered, "Mother and Father don't want me calling, but something is wrong."

"Who is this? Are you okay?" Dee heard the squeak of metal on metal. "Hello? What's your—"

She heard someone in another room yelling, but couldn't tell what was said.

"Miss Owens," the caller whispered, "you must find out who is pretending to be Josie."

"Pretending? What makes you think—"

The caller was gone.

Dee stared at the phone, willing it to ring again. Surely the caller would phone back. She had to. Dee needed more information.

Josie? Racking her brain, Dee recalled a girl in her dorm with the name Josie. What was her last name? Were there other Josies at Magnolia College ten years ago?

There was something familiar about the caller's voice. Logically speaking, it could be any well-bred Southern woman, but Dee couldn't shake the feeling that they knew each other.

She waited a few moments, hoping the mystery woman would call again. When it was clear that wasn't going to happen, Dee logged into the Web site and reread all of the posts. The only Josie to leave a message hadn't given a last name. Dee had assumed at the time it was from the Josie she remembered, but maybe there had been another Josie enrolled at Magnolia College. The post said Josie had taken a whirlwind tour of Europe after graduation and mentioned a daughter. But why would someone pretend to be someone else on a college reunion Web site? And why was this caller so sure it wasn't the real Josie? Maybe it was simply a case of mistaken identity.

While she was logged on, Dee searched the Web site, wondering how the caller had gotten her contact information. Unless this was the person who'd hacked into the site and found Dee's name as the administrator, she had no clue how she could have known. After another hour, Dee finally gave up waiting to hear back from the frantic woman.

Grabbing her belongings again, she went down the back stairs of the administrative building, toward Kessler Library, noticing the new memorial garden that Cassie Winters had planted after her brother's murder. She also noted the new emergency phones dotting the sidewalks across campus.

Walking past the new library's construction site,

Dee felt an odd sense of stepping back in time, to her own college days again, when they'd all felt perfectly safe walking across campus any time of day. All that had changed with recent events.

The air smelled like rain, bringing back memories of dashing to class, soaking wet.

She felt a few raindrops and walked faster.

She'd never liked studying at the library. Something about the huge old building gave her the chills. That feeling was heightened now, since a body had been uncovered on the library's grounds.

Maybe it was just that she was thinking so much about the skeleton lately, who the victim was, and what she'd gone through. Not fifty feet from where she stood, Dee realized. Glancing over her shoulder, Dee noticed a dark shadow behind the row of azaleas that Cassie had planted in the memorial garden.

She picked up her pace, her heels clicking on the sidewalk. As a chill went up her spine, Dee looked to the left, then the right. The few students out walked in groups, ducking under trees to stay dry. All except one person—a short and slight figure wearing a dark, hooded sweatshirt. The person turned away from her, then walked toward the music school. Dee let out a sigh of relief. Even though the campus was well lit, she still had an eerie feeling. Her imagination was probably getting the best of her, she told herself. Just in case, when she was done at the library, she'd call the campus security office and request an escort to take her back to her car, another of the changes the college had put into place recently.

She replayed the phone conversation over in her mind, focusing hard to think of something she'd missed. The woman had had a very strong Southern accent and a formal speech pattern. But that was little help—Georgia was full of women with Southern accents.

Dee glanced back at the music building as she went up the steps to the library. She didn't spot anyone, though it was difficult to see much with the lush undergrowth of palmettos and Spanish moss hanging from the live oak.

After stepping through the heavy oak doors, she passed the front desk. "Ma'am, would you scan your campus ID card?"

Dee kept an eye on the entrance as she dug through her purse for her wallet. "I know it's here somewhere."

The student working behind the desk said, "If you don't have it with you, I need to have you fill out a community ID. It's part of our new security policy."

"I just got a new card—I hope it's in this purse." With a sigh of relief, Dee pulled her staff ID card from her wallet and brushed it past the scanner. "Are the yearbook archives still in the basement?"

"Yes, ma'am."

Dee hurried downstairs. At a table in a quiet corner facing the exit, Dee piled decade-old school yearbooks and newspapers from when she attended Magnolia College around her and started through them, recalling events she'd almost forgotten.

She laughed quietly at the costume contest pictures

from her freshman year. The girls on her dorm floor had gone in the pajama party theme. She and Steff Kessler wore their freshly curled hair in banana clips on the back of their heads. Jennifer Pappas had her toothbrush tangled in dental floss hanging around her neck like a necklace; Josie Skerritt's curling iron was twisted and dangling from her hair. That was her last name—Skerritt! Trying to place the other girls in the photo, she looked closer. Payton…Payton Bell and Alicia Whittaker.

Dee knew from the e-mails that Josie hadn't been at the reunion, but was Payton there? That was her only regret about the reunion: she'd spent so much time with Edgar that she hadn't really talked to anyone else there, besides her closest friends. She smiled. It had been a wonderful night.

Now, looking through the old photos, she couldn't believe how much they had all changed. It took her a moment to find Cassie Winters in the group photo. Who was that in the baby-doll pajamas? Penny Brighton. And next to her, Kate Brooks dressed in footie pajamas and bunny slippers with her hair in knots all over her head. They'd nearly caused a riot on campus with their outrageous ideas. But they had won the gift certificate which allowed them to order pizza a couple of nights. Pure gold in those days.

Suddenly she stopped reminiscing. The body had been buried ten years ago. *The skeleton could be one of us,* she realized. She pulled her PDA from her bag and started a list of classmates and who she'd known in the photos, along with the issues of the newspapers.

She hoped someone's picture or name would leap out at her and remind her of the mystery caller's voice. She noticed another photo of Josie and Payton and added them to her lengthy list.

After an hour of skimming through several old newspapers, Dee wondered if she should skip the search and call the police with her list. Then again, Detectives Anderson and Rivers had pretty much dismissed her when she reported the flames over their reunion picture. Dee was hesitant to go to them again without strong proof. She still couldn't believe she'd accidentally deleted it from the server. Without actual evidence, the police didn't have anything to work with.

As she picked up another newspaper, her stomach growled. Dee checked at her watch and considered running to get a bite of supper, but decided that by the time she walked to her car, drove over to Burt's Pizza, then back, she'd waste at least an hour. The library didn't close for four more hours, and she knew she wouldn't sleep a wink if she didn't figure out who had called. She hated to let this go even another day. She'd find a snack machine and see if they had something semihealthy to get her through another hour or two.

Dee headed up the back stairs on her search for food. The hallway was dim and quiet, reminding her again why she'd never studied here. She liked noise, felt a sense of security in crowds. The soft voices and pages turning here did nothing to soothe her nerves.

Neither did the dark-haired woman in the black sweatshirt standing outside the main entrance.

Was that the same person I saw outside? From

this angle, she couldn't tell for sure if the woman's sweatshirt was hooded. The woman didn't seem to notice Dee, so she hurried back to the lower level—chocolate bar and a bottle of iced tea in hand, annoyed at her own paranoia.

The research section seemed emptier than it had been when she arrived. The library assistant was nowhere to be seen, or heard. Dee clutched her purse a little closer and opened the next newspaper.

Soon she was distracted by a feature article on Edgar. She forgot about the lack of noise and barely heard footsteps at the next table. She glanced up to see a young woman set a book on the table and sit down to read.

Dee glanced quickly at the picture of Edgar with longer hair and moved on to the article. No wonder she'd never met him in college. He had come to the United States as a missionary of sorts. His church had sponsored his trip to the States and he'd lived off campus with the pastor's family.

She thought back to the reunion, when she'd finally met Edgar....

"Lauren Owens, I'm glad you could make it tonight." Edgar had greeted them as they came in the door. He smiled at her sister, but his eyes caught Dee's and he paused.

Lauren smiled back and flung her arms around his broad shoulders. "It's not like I came all the way from Brazil for the reunion! What are you doing now, Edgar?"

"I'm living here in Magnolia Falls, for starters. I'm in the process of naturalization."

Dee had intervened. "You're the assistant director of admissions, now, aren't you?" She'd seen his picture in the *Gazette* a while back. It was impossible to miss a picture of Edgar, ten years ago, or now. She'd seen him on occasion at business events, but somehow their paths hadn't crossed in school or now.

He glanced at Dee and offered his hand. "I am. You must be Lauren's sister. Lauren, why didn't you ever introduce your sister and me?"

"Didn't I?" Lauren pretended to be puzzled, but Edgar simply laughed.

"I wouldn't have forgotten someone so beautiful." Edgar's grasp was warm and firm, not bone crushing like most men she worked with. He kissed the back of Dee's hand, and she couldn't help but smile.

Typical Brazilian, suave and macho, wrapped in a to-die-for package. Too bad he's wasting all this charm on me. I'm tired of the love-'em-and-leave-'em type.

Lauren leaned close to Edgar and whispered intentionally loud enough for Dee to hear. "That's because she doesn't like to be noticed for her looks. Dee is a brilliant public relations specialist."

"She exaggerates," Dee said with slight embarrassment.

"Forgive me for noticing the obvious, Dee. Lauren used to tell us you couldn't join us on Sunday nights because you were studying. She was always very proud of you."

Dee had stopped going to church after the pastor mishandled counseling family and friends through her best friend's illness. She recalled how, after calling in the pastor, Annie's parents had refused treatment for her cancer, insisted if they had enough faith, God would heal her. She'd watched Annie fade away. Dee had been angry at the parents, at the church members for not intervening, and at God. Surely God hadn't given doctors the wisdom to heal if He'd meant for humans to turn their back on medical care. She let out a sigh and felt the familiar old emptiness. Her sister had tried to convince her that being a Christian didn't mean using one's faith as a crutch. That had been a decision made by one family. Everyone made mistakes, she realized.

Before Dee could respond, Jennifer Pappas joined their group. "I'm sorry to intrude. Edgar, Dee, it's so good to see you both here. Lauren, could you help me with something?"

"We'll catch up later." Lauren gave Edgar another quick hug then dashed off to the foyer of Moss Hall, leaving Dee awkwardly alone with him.

"It's good to see everyone again." Edgar's gaze settled on Dee. "Could I get you a drink?"

Why hadn't she taken her chance to escape with Lauren and Jennifer? She'd never known him in school, and now it would be awkward to just walk away and leave him there alone. Edgar seemed nice, but…there was something she just couldn't quite figure out about him.

"I'd love some mineral water." She heard herself say.

"With a lemon?" Edgar said.

"With lemon would be wonderful." Dee followed him, surprised that Edgar had left his assignment on the welcoming committee. "I understand the school will be conducting a search for a new director of admissions soon. I presume you have put your name into the running?"

Edgar shrugged as if it wasn't a big deal. "I'm still thinking on the subject. There's much to consider before taking such a position."

"So you aren't interested?" Dee inquired, noting that his English was so proficient that she'd forgotten it was not his native language. It didn't make sense that Edgar would pass up an opportunity like that when he already had a foot in the door. "*Director* would look very good on a résumé, even if it is at a small college. Magnolia College has an outstanding reputation nationally, which I'm sure you're very aware of."

Edgar smiled with an overdose of confidence. "I am, but I'm more than happy that you share my opinion. What did you like most about Magnolia College?"

Little had she known that their chance meeting would end up landing her a job with the college weeks later. She'd definitely enjoyed the evening. They'd eaten dinner together and continued their conversation.

Edgar had proved a puzzle to Dee, and she regretted her initial opinion of him. In one respect, he was no different than most of the businessmen she met— out to sell and charm. In her line of work, the majority of the men were more concerned with appearances than they were sincerity or honesty.

With Edgar there was a difference, though. He could pour on the charm, but she still sensed his integrity. He believed in Magnolia College, heart and soul.

In the weeks since, he had both surprised and disappointed her. At first, she thought she'd felt a personal interest from him, but there again, she'd been wrong. It appeared now that he was only interested in her professional expertise. In that regard, his determination had been overwhelmingly flattering. He had called her a month after their reunion, asking her if she would come to the college to discuss the skeleton incident and give her opinion on reversing the damage. Next thing she knew, he'd managed to get her hired on a temporary contract, not an easy feat with all the red tape of a college. And then his flirting had ended.

She missed it.

Dee closed the article on Edgar, understanding his love for Magnolia College a little better. It had given him the chance to succeed in America and the means to provide a better life for his family. Yet the more Dee learned about Edgar, the more she wanted to get to know *everything* about him. And despite him pushing her away, Dee was determined to figure out why.

FOUR

"What are you doing here this late?" a man whispered.

Dee gasped, startled from her reverie. Who was talking? Where was he? She spun around, not seeing anyone; she realized just how alone she was in the library basement.

"Over here." A man's eyes shone through the books on the other side of the shelf.

She dropped the yearbooks and ran toward her table.

The man stepped out of the next aisle and blocked her escape. "Dee, it's just me, Edgar. Did I really frighten you?"

Her hands were bunched into fists as she looked up. "Edgar," she whispered. She nearly collapsed from the relief, steadying herself against the heavy oak chairs. "I didn't hear anyone come into the room." She felt her face warm. "I was just..." Her voice faded away.

He wrapped an arm around her and she let out a

huge sigh. "I'm sorry. I really did scare you, didn't I? I thought you'd seen me. Forgive me, please." He held her close. "Your heart's beating like crazy. What's happened?" he asked.

Dee pushed herself away from him as she inhaled the scent of his spicy aftershave. "I've just been…" She couldn't tell him she'd been reading, let alone daydreaming, about him. Her attention went to his strong shoulders—usually hidden beneath a suit jacket—now straining against the fabric of his polo shirt.

"You were just, what?" He studied her intently. "Are you sure you are okay?"

"Oh, yeah," she said, freeing herself from his warm embrace. "I'm a little on edge tonight, I guess. I was just looking through old yearbooks."

"Need a few laughs, huh?"

She pressed her lips together and nodded. Slowly, she added, "I wish it were just that. No, I was looking for someone who has been on our missing alumni list."

Edgar touched her shoulder. "What's wrong?"

Dee shrugged. "Nothing, really. Did you get my message about the ideas Steff and I came up with?"

Edgar looked puzzled. "Did you leave it at the office?"

She didn't want to appear needy or weak. "Yes, but we don't need to discuss it tonight. We can go through it Monday," she said stubbornly backing away.

"Whatever it is, it's upset you." His dark eyes sought hers. "Dee, what happened?"

Between thinking of him, the phone call, and the suspicion that someone had followed her into the library, she felt frazzled and confused. "I'll be fine," she stammered. "It's nothing I need to bother you with. We'll discuss the ideas Monday."

"Edgar," a young woman called out. "I can't find anything on the existence of…" The young woman's voice sounded familiar. Then again, so did the caller from earlier. Dee turned, surprised to see his younger sister, Christiana. She felt like she really was losing it tonight.

"Last-minute homework," Edgar said with a shake of his head.

Christiana saw Dee and smiled. "I'm sorry. I didn't realize you were talking with Miss Owens."

Relieved it wasn't the woman in the dark sweatshirt, Dee answered, "Hello Christiana. What are you working on?"

"Where Magnolia Falls got its name."

Dee forced a laugh when she really wanted to cry tears of relief. "If you find out, let me know. I've always wondered that, too." They spent a few minutes surmising how the founders had come up with the ill-fitting name for a town with no falls. Dee felt the emptiness in her stomach. "I'd better call it a night. It was good to see both of you."

Edgar must have read her mind, for he grabbed her wrist as she rushed past. "Dee," he said. He suddenly turned to Christiana. "Honey, go get your books. We're going to run out of time to take you to Julia's house if we don't get going."

Dee tried to ignore the warmth of Edgar's hand gently holding hers. Before she'd been hired, she'd briefly daydreamed of him holding her hand, sharing dreams, laughing together. But that had quickly come to an end. Edgar was all business. They hadn't had a personal conversation since they'd begun working together.

Christiana glanced at her watch. "We have an hour."

"Then why don't we go to Burt's for pizza. Dee, we'd love for you to join us, wouldn't we, Christiana?"

"Of course. I'd like to talk to you more about public relations. I saw you on the news the other night. You make it look so easy. Do you think the police know who the killer is?"

"Later, Christiana," Edgar reminded her, tapping his watch.

Dee took a deep breath and waited for Christiana to get out of earshot. "I appreciate the invitation, but I should get home."

"What I want to say is that you shouldn't be walking around campus at night by yourself. You're putting yourself in great danger. Everyone wants to know what you know, Dee. And apparently, they think we at the college know everything that's going on. You should be more careful."

She couldn't hide her surprise. "Don't pretend to be concerned for me, Edgar. You couldn't even stand to stay through the press conference."

"What?" he exclaimed as he spotted Christiana. "I

don't want to talk about this in front of my sister, but we need to clear this up."

"That can be done on Monday," she said. Right now, she wanted to get to her car and go home where she could relax.

Dee was about to leave herself, when Edgar gave her one of his to-die-for smiles. "And who is walking out now?"

FIVE

Edgar realized he shouldn't have been so blunt with Dee about the danger of her walking outside alone, but she shouldn't be running around at night, not after all that had been happening. "I'm sorry, Dee."

"Thank you, but..." she began, then turned away. "I've had a long day, and I'm sorry I snapped at you. It's not really you I'm upset with."

"Wait for us so we can walk you to your car," Edgar said. "Christiana, are you ready?"

Christiana sent him a puzzled look. "As soon as I check these out." While his sister waited in line to check out her books, Edgar led Dee to a far corner, so they could talk quietly.

"I'm not sure what is really going on Dee, but something has clearly been bothering you since the press conference. At least now I know what I did to upset you."

She looked at Christiana, then back at Edgar. "You hired me to spin the damage, but then you couldn't stand to stay and listen. Why couldn't you have put up a united front for the press, or at least be supportive?"

"You're a professional, you've never seemed like the type to want someone to hold your hand while you did your job. I knew what you had to report—and I trusted you to do that without watching over you."

He was right. And it annoyed her even more. She took a step closer and tilted her head toward his. "I've never had to spin the attempted murder of my friends, either," she whispered through tight lips. "Not to mention I still think the attacks on my sister a few weeks ago and the vandalism at my own carriage house are related to this mess somehow. But I'm supposed to make the school look good, so I did my best. One friendly face would have helped. But you're right, I am a professional, and I will take care of business. Alone."

He'd never realized that Dee was struggling with this. Edgar wanted more than ever to take this beautiful woman into his arms and protect her. At the reunion, he was sure they'd made a personal connection. But he never mixed business with pleasure. "It's complicated, but it had nothing to do with how you're handling the job, Dee. I'm sorry if I gave you that impression." He briefly touched her arm, then let his hand drop to his side. Dee was still angry, but whether it was at him or something else, he wasn't sure. "So, before Christiana gets back here, what's happened tonight? And don't tell me that it's nothing." He placed a finger on her chin and turned her to face him.

He could see moisture in her eyes as she blinked,

trying to hide her reaction. "It's probably just my imagination," she said hesitantly, until he leveled her with a look of reproach.

"Don't lie."

She turned her head, forcing his hand away. "Steff and I spent the entire afternoon coming up with ideas on how to pull in the alumni to help recruiting. I was waiting for you to return my call when I received a very strange call."

"About what?"

Christiana stepped up to the counter and the clerk began processing her books.

"There isn't time to go into detail now. I'm sure you don't want to talk about the skeleton, assault, vandalism and attempted murder around your sister."

"No, I don't, thank you. If you can wait until I drop Christiana at a friend's house, we'll be able to talk it all out. I know this is getting complicated."

Dee nodded. "I just can't help but wonder if the woman was someone I knew. When I was leaving the office, my phone rang. I hoped it was you, so I went back inside and answered it. We had a bad connection, and I couldn't make out everything she said, then we were cut off. I waited a while, in case she called back. I walked over here to do some research and I was sure I saw someone hiding in the palmettos… then you startled me. You know how creepy these live oaks get during a storm with the moss swaying and all."

He smiled sympathetically. "All the more reason you shouldn't be out by yourself tonight. Whether you eat anything or not, you're coming with us and I'm going to make sure you're home safe."

She looked like she was going to put up a fight, then suddenly agreed. "Okay."

He was surprised. "Good. Then maybe I can make up for not showing my support the other day. Whether or not you believe me, I do feel responsible for getting you involved. I'm the one who begged you to be our public relations spokesman. I pushed you into this role, and if that brings you harm, I won't forgive myself."

"Oh! That's it!" Dee burst out, making everyone nearby look at them. "Of course! Thank you, Edgar."

He held out his hand to hush her, then whispered, "Why are you thanking me? If someone is following you…"

"No, that's not what I mean." She lowered her voice. "About that weird phone call I received earlier tonight. I thought the person called me because of the Web site. I couldn't figure out how she knew to call me, why she didn't just e-mail the Webmaster. But of course, she must have seen me in the news conference on Monday."

"What was this call about?"

Christiana returned with her books loaded into her backpack. "I'm ready."

Edgar forced a smile and wrapped an arm around both Dee and Christiana, saying a silent prayer for God to protect these women when he couldn't. "So, what kind of pizza do you ladies desire?" He didn't want to worry his sister any more than these scandals already had.

"I like any kind. Where should I meet you? Burt's?" Dee asked, her independent nature a reflex for her.

Edgar shook his head. "I think you should ride over with us, then we'll bring you back to your car."

"That's not…"

Dee just was not going to adjust easily to letting someone help her. From what he had learned from Lauren, Dee had been a driven and independent woman even in college. Time hadn't changed that. "I won't have it any other way," he countered sternly. "With all of the warnings the campus police have issued about not walking across campus alone, I think the administration needs to follow those rules as well. Safety in numbers. Remember that."

Dee glanced at Christiana, and quickly agreed. "You're right. This is so difficult to change the way I do everything. So Christiana, what grade did you get on the career-shadowing project?"

"Pretty good, I ran out of time with writing my report, but I still got a B+. I had so much I wanted to say about what a cool job you have."

Dee laughed and raised a brow to Edgar. "And what is this new project about?"

As they walked out of the building, Christiana told Dee all about her history research. Meanwhile Edgar kept an eye out for anyone who may have been following Dee. The rain had tapered off to a light drizzle. Dee was right, rain did make an old campus seem a little more frightening on a dark night.

He noted a couple of people walking alone, but no

one looked out of place. And no one seemed to be watching Dee. He sincerely hoped she was imagining things, but he wasn't about to take any chances.

After a lighthearted meal, filled mostly with Christiana and Dee's chatter, Edgar invited Dee to come by his condo to discuss work.

"Why don't we talk Monday?" she suggested instead. "I'm sure everything will seem less dramatic in the daylight."

Edgar escorted Christiana and Dee to his black sports car and opened the door for his sister, closing her inside.

"I'm worried about you," Edgar said quietly.

"You shouldn't be," Dee argued. "You offered to take me to my car. I appreciate that, and I'm not arguing the point." She reached for the handle of the front door.

His hand pressed firmly against hers, holding the door closed. "If you won't come by my condo, let me follow you home, please. I need to know more about this phone call, Dee."

"If Monday's not early enough, then tomorrow," she begged. "I'm exhausted. And I know you don't want to worry Christiana."

Edgar took hold of her free hand. "It's not only my sister I'm concerned about. Jameson King never found out what Scott Winters called him about, and the next day, Scott was dead. Strange things are happening in Magnolia Falls. Tomorrow may not come. Tonight would be far better."

"You're being cruel."

"No, I'm being realistic," he said.

Fear, stark and vivid, glimmered in her pale blue eyes. She yanked her hand out of his, pushed him away and climbed into the car.

SIX

Up the street from Burt's Pizza, the watcher stared in confusion as Dee argued with some hunk outside his black sports car while a young woman sat in the backseat. *What's wrong, Dee? Lover's spat, or are you afraid of little old me?* Pulling up the hood of the sweatshirt, she looked both ways before slipping out of her hiding place in the alley. She pushed the black-framed glasses up on her nose. *What on earth were you looking for in the library, you nerd? You always did have your nose in a book.* The watcher glanced up the street to the library. *If only they hadn't put in that stupid security system, I could get inside and figure out what you're onto. The last thing I need is you sticking your nose in my business. I'll make sure you keep your mouth shut, and I know just how to do it.*

Dee watched as Edgar walked around to the front of the car minutes after scaring her back to her senses with his "I'm being realistic" comment. She wasn't too happy with him.

Christiana sighed. "I hate when Edgar gets like this. Our father was very protective, too. It's a genetic flaw in Brazilian men."

Dee couldn't help but laugh at Christiana's analysis of her brother. "It's as endearing as it is annoying, but in this case, he's right. We all need to be extra careful," she said, clipping her comment as Edgar opened the driver's-side door and sat down.

"Christiana, we're going to take you by Julia's, then I'm going to make sure Miss Owens gets home okay. I want you to call if you need anything. I don't care how late it is."

"Whatever," she said, as if he were punishing her by making her stay at a friend's house. Dee expected Christiana to argue, but she didn't.

"It's really not necessary for you to take me home, Edgar."

"It's not a problem," he insisted.

Dee resigned herself to going along with Edgar's plan. For the time being anyway. She was tired, and she really didn't want to go home alone. With Lauren in Savannah for the weekend, going home to a dark, empty house held little appeal after Lauren had been attacked in her backyard. She couldn't deny that it felt comforting to know he was next to her, just in case anyone was watching.

They arrived at Julia's and Edgar walked his sister to the door. Dee watched Edgar step inside and be greeted by a middle-aged man she presumed to be

Julia's father. Knowing Edgar, she imagined he was apologizing for the inconvenience.

Her mind drifted back to the phone call. The more she thought about it, the only voice that came to mind was Josie Skerritt. But why would Josie call to say the messages were from an impostor? Why couldn't one thing in this entire scandal make some sort of sense?

A few minutes later, Edgar returned to the car. "Sorry for the delay, Dee," he said. "I wanted to make sure Julia's parents understand why I'm a little more concerned than usual."

"I'm sorry to cause all of this trouble, but now I'll admit, I'm relieved to have someone with me."

"Good." Edgar reached over the console and took hold of Dee's hand. "I wouldn't forgive myself if you'd said no. Where are you parked?"

"In K lot, near the bell tower." She noted that he wasn't letting go of her hand, and she didn't mind. It was a nice reminder of the reunion, when she'd thought he was flirting with her. "It's not your fault, the extra exposure, I mean. It goes with the profession. And it doesn't normally bother me. But it does feel more personal with this job. If Lauren wasn't out of town this weekend, I'd at least have her waiting at home for me. I should…" her voice faded as she thought of what had already happened in town over the past few months. "Before you leave me at my car, I want to tell you about the call, just in case."

"I apologize. I didn't mean to scare you by bringing up Scott's death."

"It's true, though. The police would know what story he was researching if his laptop had been found or if he'd left Jameson more information, and we'd probably know who killed him by now. I'm not so much worried about myself as I am hoping we catch this maniac before anyone else is hurt." Dee told him about the mysterious call. "I searched the Internet for a Josie Skerritt, but there were no results on any of the sites or search engines."

"That's very strange," Edgar said thoughtfully.

It felt better knowing someone else was concerned. She realized that she really should write it all down while it was fresh in her memory, in case it did turn out to be important information that the police might need.

"And she didn't give any clue as to who she is?" Edgar turned into the parking lot, made a circle and left the parking lot again. "Do you have any premonition of who it could be? Who were Josie's friends in college? Who would he have kept in touch with?"

"Premonitions?" Dee laughed. "I don't have premonitions. Or at least I don't think I do. And who is the 'he' you're thinking of?" Dee noticed Edgar going around the block for a second time. "Edgar, you just went by my car. Where are you going?"

"I was busy talking and want to take another look around in the landscaping. When I get nervous I confuse my pronouns and mix up my languages. Sorry."

It endeared Edgar Ortiz to her even more. Macho, chivalrous, and he didn't hesitate to admit he was a bit frightened, too. Now she was really scared. She forced herself to think of the caller to ease her concern about getting into her own car.

"I was so focused on the caller's voice that I didn't really consider who Josie would've kept in touch with. Now all I can think of is that the voice sounds like Josie's did." She let out a deep sigh and shook her head. "But if it was Josie, why wouldn't she have just said someone was responding as her? The more they dig into this case, the more peculiar it's getting." Edgar circled once more before returning to her car. Then he made her wait until he'd looked around it before allowing her to get in.

"I'll follow a little too close. If you see anything that alarms you, pull over in a busy place. And keep your phone handy. And…"

"Edgar, you're scaring me even more. Let's get on the road. And you do realize that I live half an hour out of town, don't you?"

He paused. "Since your other office is in Savannah, I didn't think you lived around the corner, but no, I don't know exactly where your apartment is. It's okay, I'll follow. I'm not going to send you out there alone."

"Okay, don't say I didn't give you a chance to back out. And, just so you know, it's a house, out by the Magnolia Lane Golf Course." She watched in amazement as he hurried back to his car. His broad shoulders were enough to scare that puny stalker away, she was sure of that. She glanced into the shadows, relieved that no one was looking back.

Twenty-six minutes later, Dee pulled into the long driveway to her two-story home, wondering how she could be certain that no one was lurking outside. She turned her headlights on bright, then entered the security code to open the garage door. She pulled in on one side, motioning for Edgar to pull into the other. After they were both inside, Dee closed the garage door and breathed a sigh of relief. She got out of her car and entered the security code on the garage entry to the house.

Edgar looked around, a smile softening his strong jaw. "Impressive." He met her at the door and glanced around. "Do you have a baseball bat or something?"

"Closest thing is a golf club. It's over there." Dee pointed to the storage cabinets on the far side of the garage. "They came with the house."

Edgar raised an eyebrow. "You golf?"

"When I have to, let's just say it's not a problem letting the client win." She smiled. "Come on. It's going to be fine. After that jealous student broke into my carriage house to scare Lauren away from Seth, I had a security system installed. The service would have called if there'd been any problems. Would you like some coffee? I won't guarantee it's as good as in Brazil, but…"

"You are a beautiful surprise, Deandra. Here we are scared out of our wits and you're going to make coffee, and worry that I won't like it." He motioned toward the door.

Dee laughed as she returned the key to her purse, more than a little relieved to be home. "No one calls me Deandra," she said in a light tone. Edgar stepped inside ahead of her. "That's not fair," Dee said, playfully tugging on his arm. "I don't get to see your reaction to my home if you're ahead of me."

Thunder rumbled. Edgar stopped suddenly and pulled her into his embrace.

SEVEN

He'd been outside waiting since the sun went down. He'd crawled through foot-high weeds to get to Dee's house from the back side of the golf course, where he'd hidden that dump of a car he'd found in an Atlanta newspaper. It was cheap, and no paperwork to trace the sale. Just what he needed right now, something to get around in unnoticed.

He eyed the approaching thunderstorm, hoping it passed quickly without dumping too much rain. He'd been sitting in her gazebo, waiting for the call.

If it got too muddy, he'd leave tracks right back to the car. He'd have to duck into the garage and surprise her after she turned off that blasted security system. He tugged on the wire leading from the house to the pole out back, ready to run at a moment's notice if an alarm went off. Nothing. It was better news than he'd hoped for. It had to have disconnected something.

I'd have thought you'd be smarter than this, Ms. Owens. Especially after all those close calls with Lauren.

Lightning cracked, hitting the tree next to him, sending a branch to the ground.

Then again, a thunderstorm could also hide evidence. *How much more perfect could this be?*

He picked up the branch and placed it over the downed wire. Just a little mishap with Mother Nature. His black clothes were getting soaked, and the leather gloves were going to dye his hands black if they got wet. He'd never be able to explain that to his wife. He tugged them off and tucked them into his pocket.

Where in the world is she? He felt his cell phone vibrate. All looked quiet here. He took the phone from his pocket and answered quietly.

"She's on her way home, finally. I had her trapped in the library, when she met up with some guy and a girl. Don't miss this time."

"Don't threaten me again." He glanced at his watch and ended the call. *It'll take her at least twenty minutes, maybe more.* While he waited, he went through everything one more time, making sure he hadn't missed anything. Half an hour later, he heard a car approach, ducked around the corner of the garage and hid behind the azalea bush, ready to crawl inside behind her car.

But two sets of headlights pulled into her driveway, and he was surprised to see a sports car follow her into the garage. He'd seen that car on campus.

Why didn't you tell me she was going to have company?

He backed away, deeper into the shrubs, and waited for them to get inside. First the garage door closed, then he heard the inside door bang shut. Thunder rumbled overhead. He turned and ran, straight into the fallen branch.

EIGHT

"I'm sorry," Edgar said with a grimace as they knocked heads. He pressed his finger against her lips and listened. They were both silent for a moment, which felt like hours to Dee. "I thought I heard something," he whispered. He saw a flash of lightning, then thunder rumbled again. "I guess it's just the storm. I'm sure your home is as beautiful as you are."

Dee blushed. "Edgar... Please don't say that."

"No one seems to call you beautiful, either, but I seem to get away with it on a regular basis," he said with quiet emphasis. "Inside and out, you're a very special woman, Dee." He looked at her with such admiration, she couldn't argue. It wasn't the same look other men gave her.

He cared about her, or he wouldn't have gone to so much trouble to make sure she was safe, she told herself. Dee felt her heart race. She looked into Edgar's dark eyes and waited for him to pull her closer. The clock ticked away the seconds as Edgar stared back. She hoped she wasn't imagining something that wasn't really happening.

"I'm going to regret this," he mumbled as he pulled her toward him and his lips touched hers.

Glass shattered in the next room. Edgar forced Dee to the ground, ducking behind the kitchen counters. "Shh," he whispered in her ear.

Dee felt the cold, hard Italian tile against her back. Edgar's warm strong arms closed in around her. Into her mind flashed the quick thought that this wouldn't be a bad way to die—in his arms.

She wanted to cry. Was someone after her? When would this end?

They heard muffled noises, like someone tiptoeing across the room. "I'm going to go see who it is. You stay here," he whispered into her ear.

She pulled him back down and tried to roll over him. "I should go," she insisted, "I know where the lights and furniture are."

"No way are you going out there." He kissed her on the forehead and jumped to his feet.

"Meow." Her cat Tipsy jumped across the counter and solidly hit Edgar's chest. He fell back onto the floor and batted the cat away.

"It's my cat," Dee said. She tried to grab the tortoiseshell cat out of the line of fire. "Tipsy, it's okay."

The cat hissed. It batted at Edgar, determined to be rid of him. Edgar rolled over and had freed himself from the critter's claws when the cat took another dive at him.

"Dee! Get him off of me."

"Hold still," she said in a forced croon, her heart racing.

"I'm trying," Edgar said through clenched teeth. The cat crawled over his shoulder and batted at the back of his neck.

"I meant the cat. But you too. Something really has her spooked."

"Something, or someone?" He started to laugh, deep and soft, even through the pain. "I don't think Tipsy is going to be my best friend."

Dee scratched Tipsy's ears, trying to ease her claws from Edgar's back. She'd thought the cat only had hold of his shirt, but apparently Tipsy had dug clear into his skin. "I think the feeling's mutual, isn't it?"

Dee stood with the cat, speaking softly as she comforted it.

"Your cat's a mind reader."

"Why?" Dee said, as she finally freed Edgar from Tipsy's sharp clenches. She held the cat close.

"I've never been particularly fond of cats, and she knows it." Edgar slid across the tile away from the cat before he stood.

"Female tortoiseshells have a neurological disorder, but Tipsy had never had an episode like this before."

"I think we should check the house out, make sure it was only the cat wreaking havoc in the other room," he said quietly.

"I think I know what she knocked over," Dee said.

"I wonder if the storm knocked your electricity out…"

Dee switched on the lights. She knew instantly what had broken, and nodded. "The alarm has a battery backup, and this security system has sensors in the window glass as well. There's no way anyone has gotten inside."

"Stranger things have happened," he said as he peeked into the next room. The windows were fine, and he came right back after seeing the turquoise glass on the tiled entry. "It looked like a vase."

"Turquoise glass?"

Edgar nodded.

"It was going to be Lauren and Seth's wedding gift, but I wasn't totally sure if she'd like the color. I don't keep too many breakables out on display because of Tipsy. She didn't get the name because she drinks too much. Let me take her upstairs to my bedroom and close her in until I have time to clean it up. Then I'll make some coffee."

"Tell me where it is, and I'll get it brewing." Edgar rubbed his neck, keeping his eyes on the cat. "Heaven help anyone who tries to sneak in here."

"I'm so sorry, Edgar. She doesn't usually do this, but if you want to announce that I have a guard tiger cat, I won't dispute your claim. I could use all the help I can get this year." She peeked back into the kitchen. "Coffee is in the canister next to the French press there. Just put water in the teakettle and turn on the stove, and I'll be right back." Dee ran up the stairs and returned with a first-aid kit.

She felt terrible. His arms were badly scratched and bleeding.

"I'm sorry she did this, Edgar. We need to clean those puncture wounds. Even though I keep her up-to-date on her shots, she is an outdoor cat." Dee spread open the first-aid kit, her hands shaking.

"You're going to hurt me as much as Tipsy, aren't you?"

Dee froze with the antiseptic bottle and cotton in her hand, then she saw the smirk on his face. "That's it, twist the knife a little more, like I'm not already feeling guilty enough."

He flinched slightly when she dabbed the cotton to the scratches. She tried desperately to forget how close he'd been to kissing her. The teakettle whistled, giving Dee a perfect excuse to hand off the agonizing torture of treating his scratches. "Why don't you clean the rest of the cuts. I'll get the coffee brewing."

His hands lingered on hers as she handed him the cotton and antiseptic. She stepped away, wishing the teakettle had waited a few more minutes to whistle.

Dee stood facing the counter, deliberately focusing on the coffee press as she poured the water over the ground coffee. She watched the water and grounds separate and the rich aroma waft into the air. She could hardly keep her hand from shaking.

The day had been too much to handle all alone. Along had come Edgar, and she knew she was in trouble. The past few weeks of working with him had been wonderful agony. She longed to get to know him better. But for now, he was practically her boss. A boss she definitely didn't want to be attracted to.

Yet she was, and getting romantically involved with a coworker was inviting trouble....

She knew it in her mind, but in her heart she wanted to find that loophole and spin the facts. She wanted to be romanced, like Steff and Lauren and Cassie. Why was it Dee Owens was always the bridesmaid and never the bride? What was it about her that scared men away?

Edgar placed a hand on her shoulder and turned her around. "Dee?" He gazed into her eyes, and she wondered if he'd read her mind.

"Yes," she said, trying to tear her mind from her emotions.

"I think we need to talk."

NINE

"It might be best if we have our coffee at the table, yes?" Edgar suggested.

Dee couldn't deny her relief that he suggested they avoid sitting together in the living room. "Sure." Though she wanted to have someone in her life, she found herself struggling with it in the moment. "It'll just be a minute. Make yourself comfortable." She set the table with linen place mats, cups and saucers, noting that Edgar kept glancing into the living room.

"Do you mind if I take another look in the living room? I'll be happy to pick up what the cat knocked over?"

"Of course not, but I'll clean up later. That vase is the only breakable thing I'd left out—I thought it was too heavy for Tipsy to knock over. Since Lauren is spending the next couple of days packing at her place in Savannah, I figured I'd leave it out, make sure it's the right color. I guess color's the least of my worries now. I'll clean it up later." Edgar disappeared from her sight, and she found herself wondering what he thought of her home.

And wondering what his looked like. He kept tight standards of professional decor at the Admissions Office and his own office was spotless, without any personal effects or knickknacks—just school memorabilia.

She was learning that he was anything but what she had expected. He didn't think like the typical American man. Yet he was a bit less bound by convention than most foreign men she'd worked with.

He took his career very seriously. He showed up in suit and tie every day, even on school-spirit Fridays when most employees dressed casually in jeans and a polo shirt. Despite the current trend for facial hair, the shadow that appeared on his jaw around noon was gone when he returned from his lunch break. Dee thought of the pictures of him with long curls in the yearbook and newspaper from ten years ago. The one thing he hadn't given up on was his sideburns. She'd never realized how much she liked well-groomed men. "Do you take cream or sugar?" Dee asked, trying to keep herself from overthinking when it came to Edgar.

"Neither, thanks." Edgar suddenly showed up behind her. He had with him huge curved pieces of turquoise glass and set them on the counter. "It was beautiful, I imagine."

He loved using that word. She suspected it was just to see the reaction he got out of her. It was silly that the word bothered her so. Most men she'd dated seemed to think looks were all she cared about.

Dee's smile didn't come easily as she tried to get her heart to stop racing. "It was, yes. I found it at the market in Savannah last week. It's a wish jar. I wanted a unique wedding gift. I hope it isn't a sign…"

He touched her lips with his finger and his eyes captured hers. "Don't think that way. Wishes are simply whimsical hopes. They come and go, like a child's Christmas list. After the holiday is over they don't even remember what was on it. Seth and Lauren's marriage will be based on God's promises, which are much longer lasting."

She took a deep breath, inhaling his subtle cologne. "That's absolutely…" She paused, as if trying to find the right word. "That's a beautiful thought, Edgar."

He pulled her close and kissed her forehead, feeling the tension ebb from her body. "Oh, Dee. I wish I hadn't asked you to help with the PR for the college. I hate seeing what all of this worry has done to everyone. I especially hate putting you in danger." He loosened his embrace.

"We can't let this person win," Dee said, studying him. "Whoever the skeleton was, she deserves justice. This kind of thing doesn't happen here in Magnolia Falls. The shootings, corruption, it has to be connected somehow."

* * *

He could see Dee's mind spinning, yet his own thoughts were as far from the case as they could be. Her eyes were perfectly framed with long brown lashes, her lips full and tempting him to finish their interrupted kiss. A kiss that shouldn't have happened in the first place. He forced his gaze to her shiny blond hair and realized he had to stop tormenting himself. "I understand how you feel," he said, his mind more than a little distracted. "Magnolia College is like home to me. I left Brazil because I fell in love with it here."

"I'm not going to let Magnolia College become a casualty, Edgar. But it is difficult when my friends are the victims. I don't normally need my hand held, but this time, it's different from anything I've ever dealt with." Her eyes drifted closed, revealing the pain she'd found invading her world.

Lord, help me to show her that she can find strength in You. And give me the strength to resist her. Help me to tell her what I came to say.

He took hold of her hands. "Justice will come in time, even if it isn't ours, but God's time. We aren't trying to handle this alone, Dee, God's watching over us."

She eased away from him. "And how many more have to lose their lives?" She glanced at the coffee, then walked over to get it. "This started ten years ago with the murder of someone we probably knew." She motioned for him to sit down while she went to get the coffee. "What's frightening is that these threats seem to come from someone close. They seem to know what's going on, firsthand." She poured their coffee, sat down and took a sip. "Do you think it could be someone working at the college?"

He couldn't believe she'd said it aloud. He'd only thought it for the briefest moment, and only to himself. "No. I've considered it, but I don't want it to be true. I'm still having trouble believing that the basketball coach may have been involved in the point-shaving. We're a small college." He shook his head. "How could this happen here without anyone catching on? How did they keep it quiet?"

"Someone on campus has knowledge of the policies and buildings, and access to what's going on here, and who or how to avoid telling the wrong person," she reasoned. "The first warning that hit the Web site guest book said 'not everyone at Magnolia College is what they seem.'" She paused, as if expecting him to argue. "Why did they target the college, not just the town? Then the other message said to look into what Cornell Rutherford has been up to the last few years. What do you think they meant?"

"Professor Rutherford is eccentric, but he wouldn't risk losing everything. He's married to Madelain Kessler, you know. Her grandfather founded the college. Plus Cornell's one of the finalists in the search for a new president of the college. That doesn't sound like someone who is going to be terrorizing campus, does it?"

"No, but it could also motivate someone to cover up a past indiscretion." Dee took a drink of her coffee, apparently not happy with the conclusion she was coming up with, as her brows twitched. "That must be why someone is sending these messages, to discredit him. Unless there's truth in the accusations somewhere…" She shook her head as she shrugged her shoulders. "This just doesn't make sense. There has to be someone else involved. You're right, Rutherford can't be doing this himself. But he knew we were starting the Web site. Steff had mentioned it to him."

Dee pressed her fingers against her temples.

"Let it go, Dee." Edgar wanted more than anything to take her into his arms again and offer some comfort, but he knew that would only make it more difficult to leave. Until this was over, he had to put his interest in Dee aside. "Those posts to the guest book were pretty direct. The police are working on it and surely they've checked into Rutherford by now."

"Someone has already threatened Lauren more than once. Someone killed Scott. The police know that the point-shaving has been going on for at least three years. Maybe longer. Last week Cassie, Jameson and Kevin Reed were shot at, too. I don't see the coach masterminding all of this. Besides, he wasn't even here ten years ago. Maybe Coach Nelson was blackmailed and forced—"

"Now that's a stretch. It could also be a coincidence," he said, keeping the silent doubt to himself. He had come tonight to make sure she made it home safely, not stir up her imagination. "Dee, you're going to get upset all over again and never go to sleep if you don't stop thinking about this." He pushed her blond hair off her face, realizing he was breaking every professional rule being there at all, let alone kissing her and wondering if she felt half as strongly about him.

"Reese trashed my guest house when Lauren was staying with me. It didn't seem so strange until I found out she's a student of Rutherford. Is that another coincidence?"

He felt a tingle go up his spine as he pulled his hand away from Dee's face. "You need to leave this to the police, Dee."

"I am letting them handle it. They know all of this, and they don't seem to be getting anywhere. He's either a very convincing actor, or…"

"Or innocent, and has a very conniving enemy out there who wants to discredit him. Either way, Dee, we can't do anything about it. We're not the police. And I hope that you're not using the college system to do your own investigations." Edgar could feel the tension in the room rise.

"Of course not. Reese told the police that she'd not been herself. She claimed she was afraid she was failing Rutherfold's class and wouldn't graduate. It's public knowledge." Dee's voice was tight.

Dee was under too much stress, personally and professionally. When they first met, Dee's beauty and ability to always look at a nearly empty glass as half-full had caught his attention. While she was still gorgeous, she had darker shadows under her eyes now. Negativity suffocated her optimism. "Leave it alone, Dee. Forget about it and let the police deal with it. Did you tell the detectives about the phone call you received tonight?"

"Not yet, but I will. I wanted more details to tell them first, so I went to the library, then I ran into you, and…I know they won't make anything of it without a name. I told them about the flames on the Web site. Did they even contact you to verify what I saw?"

There was that. "No, but I've been on the road a lot this week with recruiting, and I will be a lot more this spring. I was forced to let two recruiters go."

"See what I mean? They didn't contact Cassie or Lauren about it either. They don't seem to believe any of this is in any way connected to anything else." She jumped from her chair, poured more coffee for herself and offered to give him a refill.

He imagined it was going to be a long night and he may as well accept. "Is it decaf?"

"No, I kind of figured that would be like serving instant tea to a Brit."

He let out a laugh. He loved Dee's wit. "Bring it on, though I still wish you'd let me change the subject and get your mind off all of this, even just for the evening."

Her laugh was soft yet strained. "It was a nice idea anyway. Maybe we should see if there's a movie on. Or maybe I should tell you how tired I am and let you go home." The look in her blue eyes told him that was the last thing she wanted to tell him. She was afraid.

"Not unless you want me to leave. I'm worried about you, Dee." He knew he was walking a fine line, being here at all.

She studied him, and he couldn't take the silent questions. He stood, carried his cup to the sink and guzzled the last of his cup. "I think I'd better turn down that refill after all."

"Edgar?"

"You're right, Deandra. I should go. You're tired. Maybe sleep will help settle your nerves."

"What's that supposed to mean?" She took hold of his hand and turned him toward her. "If the scandals weren't what you wanted to talk about, what did you come all the way out here for?"

"To make sure you got home safely." He didn't dare admit how much he had grown to care for her. Not now. There were already rumors going around campus. He had to protect her honor. But tonight wasn't the best time to discuss that with her.

"What did *you* want to talk about, Edgar? You act like there's something else on your mind."

He looked into her tired blue eyes, wishing he could do anything to take away her pain. "I wanted to talk you into closing down the Where Are They

Now Web site," he said cautiously. "But I suppose that's dreaming, isn't it?"

She folded her arms and leaned against the marble counter, crossing one foot over the other. She was wearing a black wool skirt and white silk blouse that gloved her body in professionalism. "Really?" she finally said in disbelief. "Well, have your say."

"You may as well say no now and save us the time," he countered. This wasn't going well at all. How was she able to keep her mind totally on the case, when his was only on how much he wanted to tell her how he felt about her?

"I won't change my mind without a very strong reason. Maybe you'd like to see the information we've gathered about everyone before you decide." She pushed off the counter and kicked her high-heeled shoes off. "The den's off the living room. My computer is in there."

"Dee, it's late. We can discuss this Monday." Edgar followed her through the living room, past the broken wish jar. "Really, you're tired, we don't..." Edgar's argument faded when she walked through the door at the bottom of the stairs.

"This is more than a means to find missing people now, Edgar. It's bringing our classmates back together with a sense of purpose. We're remembering the idealism we had when we left college, thinking we really *could* change the world."

While the living room was formal, the den was filled with warm antiques, quilts and photographs, revealing another side of the woman he wanted to get to know better. She sat down and lifted the cover to the antique rolltop desk to reveal her laptop. While it started up, Dee pulled a delicately carved side chair with deeply tufted pink striped padding up to the desk and offered him the sturdier-looking oak desk chair.

"We've heard from a lot more people than I expected to," she said, and he could hear the optimism in her voice. This meant a lot to her.

He couldn't argue her point. He, too, had hoped he could come to America and change his life, and his sister's.

"This seems to be our best avenue to whoever's involved. It's clear that someone is angry. If it's going to help find whoever is doing this, I don't want to cut it off."

"Yes, I agree. But the link to it is on the college Web site, Dee. Parents want to see what our alumni are doing and talking about, and this is out there airing the dirty laundry. It's going to kill our recruiting."

Dee nodded, appearing genuinely concerned along with him. "I suppose I see what you mean." She thought a moment. "You know that we're also getting a lot of complaints in the newspaper about the college trying to keep unpleasantness under the rug. Taking it off the Web site will only support their accusations, and give them more to complain about. We could meet with Steff Kessler to discuss it. She'll share your concerns, and with her father on the board of trustees for the college, I'm sure her family has some opinions they've shared with her."

They browsed the new postings together, reminiscing about old times with several of their classmates. Afterward, Edgar helped her review the Internet security that Jennifer and Lauren had originally set up. Dee had added tighter protection after the hacker made it through to add the fire script, but she wasn't sure yet that it was enough.

"It really has been good to touch base with other alumni. I simply wish we could have done this long before all of this erupted," Edgar admitted, admiring the picture of her on the "Then and Now" section of the Web site she had recently added.

"Me too," she replied. "I didn't realize how much I would regret losing touch with everyone. Ten years went by like summer vacation did when I was a kid. Does that mean we're getting old?" she asked with a sleepy smile.

"No, it simply means we've grown up. Here I am raising my younger sister, and our friends are getting married," Edgar said, suddenly feeling his own age creeping up on him. "Time has flown, faster than I realized, apparently. Christiana is about ready to start college."

"It must have been difficult to take over as a parent of a teenager, but you apparently did all of the right things. Christiana is a wonderful young woman. I really enjoyed spending time with her during the career-mentoring program." Dee said, trying unsuccessfully to stifle another yawn.

"I'm afraid she thinks you have the most glamorous job now. After all of these threats, it's made me see your career in a different light. I'm not so sure I want Christiana going into public relations." *And I'm sure I don't like you being in the limelight now.*

Dee looked at him as if she could read between the lines. As if she could tell he was terrified that something was going to happen to her.

"Edgar," she said, her voice soft and oddly insecure, "I get the feeling you don't like the way I'm doing the job."

"That's not it at all, Dee," he said quickly, unsure if he was relieved.

"Then what is it?"

He could see the fatigue in her eyes, and knew it wasn't the time to get into another lengthy discussion. Thanks to the coffee, Edgar was still wide-awake, which he'd need for the drive home. "It's nothing new. I'm worried about you."

"You're right, we've been through this. I just thought there might be something else on your mind."

Edgar felt as if he was on a suspension bridge that was about to break. "I'm going to go and let you get some sleep." He stood and waited as she shut down the computer. She finished up, and he moved Dee's chair back to the corner while she put the oak chair back in place.

"I'm sorry to send you home so early after you were so kind to make sure I got home safely. But I suppose you're right. It's been a long week."

"No apology needed. You've been a perfect hostess," Edgar said. "Thank you, Dee." He waited for her to leave the room first.

She led the way back to where the garage door was, and paused in front of the door. "I can't tell you how much I appreciate you driving out here with me."

"Anytime." He couldn't miss the question in her eyes. "I hate to say this, Dee, but I hope your services aren't needed at the college for much longer. I confess, I was about to get the courage to ask you to dinner when the skeleton was found. Before I knew it, I'd missed my chance."

"If I'd been given the choice up front, we wouldn't be in this predicament." Her smile was weak at best. "I never dreamed I'd have made such a personal sacrifice for my alma mater."

He hesitated for a moment, evaluating her reaction. He had to tell her what he'd come for. "The admissions processors seem to think we're already involved with each other."

"They're very astute, or maybe prescient is a better term for them," Dee said with a playful smile. "It's a lively office, that's for sure. Much more so than I had expected. If you're worried about the kiss, I'll be discreet, I promise."

"Not all of their assumptions are flattering. I don't want any of them to get the impression that you're, well, getting preferential treatment from the administrators because of our friendship. You're far too talented to let anything stand in the way of your success."

A confident smile lit Dee's eyes and her skin flushed. "You're kidding, right?"

"That's what else I needed to talk to you about tonight."

He saw her mood fade, her anticipation fizzle. And it was all his fault. "I wanted to ask you to understand when I'm not quite as attentive at the office. In fact, it will help that I have to be out of town a few days this week for another recruiting fair."

She opened the door and stepped out of the way. "Then coming here tonight was definitely a mistake we won't let happen again." Her eyes flashed with hurt. "Be careful driving home, Edgar."

"Dee, don't think this changes how I feel."

She shook her head and closed her eyes. "I wish I was that strong."

"But you are."

"I was, before the reunion. Before these events changed all our lives. You'd think that people would be happy to see something good happening in the midst of all of this ugliness." She shook her head and distanced herself from him. "After ten years, fate brought us closer than we ever were in college. Like it did Trevor and Steff, and Lauren and Seth. Or so I hoped. And even Cassie and Jameson have found some happiness despite their sad experiences. I want to look across the office and not feel ashamed of my growing feelings for an honorable, wonderful man. And I'm just now learning to let the people I care about know that I need to know they're there for me, too. Life is too short to allow rumors to ruin something sweet and special, isn't it?"

"I don't mean this is never," he said, trying to mend the damage he'd already done. He took her hand in his and kissed the soft skin. "I hope we could see each other, date maybe after this is all over."

"You'd better go." She pressed the electric garage-door opener and waited.

"Dee," he whispered as he leaned in to kiss her. "I'm sorry."

She didn't reply, just backed away and waited for him to pull out before closing the door again. Edgar Ortiz was no different than the other men she'd dated, after all.

TEN

Dee reset the alarm system, then went to the living room and picked up the rest of the broken glass and set it inside the box—out of Tipsy's reach this time. She didn't want to make an emergency run to the vet hospital in the middle of the night. She vacuumed the room and went up to bed, listening to another thunderstorm approach.

Thoughts of Edgar's final words lulled her into a sound sleep. "Not now…"

She woke the next morning feeling much more like herself. Instead of focusing on "not now" she heard "as soon as" these threats were behind them.

Still, she didn't have the courage to go into the office Saturday and stand the chance of running into Edgar. If anyone at the college needed something, they'd call. And if the woman who had called about Josie tried again to reach Dee, maybe she'd leave a message that they could trace or understand. The late-night storm had turned off her bedside clock, and she slept well past when her alarm usually woke her. After a long ride on her stationary bicycle Dee fixed a chef salad, then cleaned out the refrigerator. She usually shopped on the weekends, but today, she just wanted to relax with a novel in the security of her own home. She glanced out to the carriage house, feeling better that there were cameras now that she could check and make sure there was direct contact between her and Lauren at a moment's notice. As Dee reheated left-overs, she flipped the button and scanned the house. Lauren's things were neatly organized, as always.

Tipsy had slept with her all night with no recur-rences of her episode. She couldn't understand what had made her attack Edgar. Usually, Tipsy was a lazy cat and perfect company.

She turned on the late news Saturday night as she got ready for bed, shocked to hear that there had been a small fire behind Burt's Pizza after they'd left Friday night. She set down her toothbrush, hurried to the television and turned up the sound, barely catching the last of the report. "Minimal damage was done to the building, and fire investigators are calling it suspicious. Investigators ask anyone with informa-tion about the incident to contact the Magnolia Falls Fire District at 555-3473."

"Well, Tipsy, do you suppose the police would believe me if I told them I was there last night right before the fire started? Or do you think they'd claim it's just another coincidence?" Tipsy purred and ran her head under Dee's hand. "Yeah, that's my thought too. Maybe Edgar's right. Maybe I just need to let the investigation go. Get it out of my head."

On Sunday, Dee woke early and finished cleaning her house before eight in the morning. She thought of her sister's constant invitations to join her at Magnolia Christian Church. Now that Lauren and Seth were engaged, Dee would feel like a third wheel, the spinster sister. Besides, Lauren and Seth were in Savannah, packing the remainder of Lauren's things to get ready to move.

Dee did go to church now and then, more out of tradition than anything else. She hated to keep disappointing Lauren, but worse than not going at all was going and not feeling the need to be there—in a holy church where believers found something that she'd apparently missed. Faith in the unseen.

Dee pulled her Bible from the shelf in the study and snuggled into the overstuffed recliner. She turned to the back cover. Tucked inside the pages of the concordance was a program from Annie's memorial service. She didn't understand to this day why they'd diluted the truth. It was a funeral. Why not call it that? Anger surfaced as if it was yesterday.

Annie's death had changed everything for her. Annie's parents had refused medical treatment for her friend's brain tumors. They'd been so sure that God would heal her if their faith was strong enough. At first, Dee had attended every prayer vigil they'd held for Annie. They'd gone to Sunday School together and lived on the same street, but the children in Annie's family attended a private school. As the illness progressed, Dee's parents said she needed to let Annie rest, and they kept Dee from seeing her best friend. Her mom and dad had both attended the services, taking her and Lauren. Dee had missed school for several days after the funeral.

Twelve-year-olds weren't supposed to die.

Dee ran her fingers over the program, reading it word for word, the one day a year that she opened her Bible. *Happy Birthday, Annie. I still miss you so much.*

Her mind wandered back to the days spent together in the backyard of their New Orleans home. Homes that were now destroyed, and families that were no longer there.

Like Annie.

She'd determined then and there that she wasn't going to use faith as a crutch, like Annie's family had. Instead of preparing themselves, they had prayed about it—put it in God's hands.

All these years she'd worked hard to become self-sufficient and responsible. To learn to handle things herself. Make decisions based upon facts and logic. Maybe Dee had been looking at this all wrong.

She had seen Annie's parents turn to God, and in Dee's eyes, God hadn't answered their prayers. They were devoted Christians, sent their children to parochial schools, went to church every week. Yet the healing they'd asked for, believed in, hadn't come. For years, she'd believed it was her fault—that because her faith wasn't strong enough, God had let Annie die. He hadn't answered *her* prayers.

Why?

Why did you let a little girl who put her entire

hope in You die, God? And why did You leave me here to wonder all these years? Why didn't I ever get an answer?

Dee ran a bubble bath, hoping maybe the daylight and warmth would melt the chill that was creeping deeper into her heart with every crisis and doubt. Surely she wasn't the only one who had ever gone through rough times when they felt alone. Even when Lauren had been attacked, she'd turned to God. Turned to her friends and Dee for strength.

Dee had never felt at a loss before, and yet now... Now she wished she hadn't studied so hard. She wished she hadn't been quite so determined to not rely on anyone else. Was that why the others were still managing to move on with their lives—because they had their faith?

What's wrong with me? Why can't I hand my fears to You like Lauren and Steff and the others do, God? Is it really a weakness to rely on someone else?

The doorbell rang, sending Dee straight into the air. Bubbles slapped her in the face and stung her eyes. Water dripped from her hair.

It rang again. Whoever it was, they were impatient. "Just give me a minute," she muttered, as if they could hear her. She slipped on the tile as she hurried to get dressed.

The person pounded on the door.

"What is the big emergency?" Dee asked.

She looked out the bedroom window, hoping she could see who was at the door. No such luck.

Dee tried to remember if she'd put the Bible back

on the shelf. If Lauren was returning from her weekend in Savannah, she didn't want her asking questions. Not yet. Then again, if it was her sister, why didn't she just use her key?

She hesitated. Looking through the peephole, Dee was surprised to see Edgar. Her first inclination was to not answer, until she realized he was probably worried about her after hearing about the fire. Ignoring him wouldn't help. Maybe something else had happened. Had someone else been hurt? She prepared herself for more bad news. "Edgar, what's wrong?" she asked as she opened the door a crack.

To her surprise, Lauren and Steff rushed around the corner of the house. "We came to make sure you're okay," Edgar responded, while her sister and Steff pushed their way inside.

"I'm fine," Dee said sheepishly, backing out of their way. She hurried to the security system and pressed the button.

"I tried calling—no one answered," Edgar said.

"I'm fine. I just needed some time to myself. It *is* a weekend."

"What happened to you? You look terrible," Lauren said.

"Thanks so much, sis."

"You've been crying," Steff Kessler exclaimed. "What happened, Dee?"

Edgar stood at the door looking as if he wanted to run.

"I have not been crying. What is such a big deal about me staying at home for a day?" She backed toward the stairway. "I was taking a bubble bath when you scared me to death. Soap got in my eyes, so that's probably why they're red."

"So you stopped answering your phone?" her sister asked. "Edgar came up to us at church and asked if we'd talked to you yesterday. He told us you'd gone to Burt's and left just before the fire Friday night. He—"

"I get the picture. But no one called."

"I called countless times," he insisted.

"I never heard the phone ring and I was here all day."

"Something's wrong then." Edgar immediately ran out the door and Dee went after him.

"What are you doing?" Dee asked, then realized she should get dressed.

"I'm holding your hand," he said as he disappeared around the corner of the house.

When Dee walked inside, she was faced with questioning looks from Lauren and Steff.

"Edgar told us about your strange phone call, and the person that you thought was watching you," Steff said. "We were terrified, Dee. We tried calling you from church…"

"I've been here for two days. Maybe the storm the other night knocked out the phone. I don't know, but it was wonderfully peaceful for a change."

"This whole thing is just getting scary. We all talked about it at church, Dee. We need to talk to the police again."

"Fine. I think that's a great idea. Maybe if we all

go in together, they'll take us seriously. Give me a few minutes and we can go. Would you see if anyone would like some coffee while I get ready?" Dee tried to shoo her sister out the door, but she'd hear none of it.

"Where's your cell phone?" Lauren demanded more than asked. "This just isn't like you, Dee. Something has to be wrong."

"I don't know where I put it. I'm sorry, Lauren." She threw her hands in the air and thought a minute. "Maybe I've reached my breaking point, I'm not sure. I just wanted some peace and quiet. I haven't made contact with anyone in two days." She went to the medicine cabinet and tried to find drops to get the red from her eyes. That was a lost cause. She put on a quick dusting of makeup and returned to her bedroom. "I read a book, from cover to cover. I cleaned the house. I actually thought about myself for a while, Laur."

"I know this has been stressful for you, Dee. You have to worry about your own safety, your friends and loved ones, and then put on a pretty face about it for the public." Lauren gave her a hug. "I've never understood how you could be so strong. Did something happen with Edgar? He's acting awfully strange, too."

Dee stopped cold. She loved her sister dearly, told her every secret she'd ever had, but she'd finally figured out that this secret didn't necessarily mean the same thing to everyone. She shook her head, not trusting herself to say anything. "I wish." Edgar's wisdom about wishes came back to mind. This was a wish she hoped didn't fade away and get forgotten.

"I'm sorry. I thought you two would hit it off. But with everything getting so creepy these last few weeks, we need to—"

"I know, I know. But aren't you just tired of living like this?" Dee asked. "I'm tired of being afraid to drive to the office, tired of being afraid what I'll find when I finally get back home. For one blissful day, life felt normal again, Lauren."

By the time they got to the bottom of the stairs, Edgar still hadn't come back inside. Steff was sitting on the sofa waiting. "You look much more like yourself, Dee. I didn't mean that the way it came out. I just thought maybe you were upset about something. Edgar seems so worried about you. I didn't realize you two…"

"We're not," Dee insisted. "He happened to run into me Friday night when I was at the library. He was just being nice. You know Edgar, he's so…"

"Old-fashioned," they all three said at once, then laughed.

Dee smiled, hoping her disappointment wasn't apparent. "He feels responsible for putting me into danger."

"Sounds like more than a guilty conscience to me," Steff said with a smile.

ELEVEN

Dee stared at Edgar as he walked back into the house. "Where'd you go?"

"To check the phone lines to the house." He wondered if Lauren and Steff would have found out about his coming to Dee's house Friday night if the fire hadn't forced them to discuss it. Dee certainly didn't look happy with him. "There's a limb down out back and a wire looks like it's torn loose." He asked if she had electricity and cable, but the phone seemed to be the only thing affected. "I guess that must be your phone line then. I thought the phone lines were mostly buried now, but something's definitely disconnected."

Dee shook her head as she walked into the kitchen. "The electricity's fine—I watched the news last night. I can't believe I didn't even notice." She picked up the receiver. "It's dead."

Steff shook her head. "Thank God nothing happened to you. We were so afraid. After Jameson and Cassie's shooting, I can't believe they haven't closed down the entire college. Every time I see Detectives Rivers and Anderson on campus, I fear the worst and at the same time I pray it's finally over."

"Who all have they talked to?" Lauren asked.

"Most of the staff in the journalism department, and of course, the athletic department," Steff replied. "Daddy is about fit to be tied."

"He's taking it much better than I expected. It's hitting everyone at the college hard," Edgar added. "When I went to visit Jameson last week, he said they've been looking into anyone with the initials *P, B,* and *R.* They aren't even waiting for the results of the tests now."

"That's an odd combination," Dee commented. "Let's see, that could be Payton Bell, or Parker Buchanan…"

"They're still waiting on the crime lab to determine whether the last name is a *B* or an *R,* so they're going ahead and investigating anyone close to those letters."

"Ten years is a long time for evidence to decay," Dee said in a tremulous whisper. "We'll be lucky if they ever solve the case."

"I'm not giving up hope," her sister said. "Speaking of which, what do you think of holding a prayer vigil?"

"I know several churches have held them, but it's never a bad idea to gather in prayer. Why don't we ask for His intervention now?" Edgar said, holding his hands out. They all joined hands. "Heavenly Father, we thank You for Your guidance and protection from the evil surrounding us. Give us wisdom and courage to stand strong against the enemy, Lord…." He paused for someone else to add to the prayer.

Steff continued, "God, I ask that You bless the missing child of the young woman whose life was so tragically cut short. Be with the detectives working the investigations, Father, and help them to find the identity, to bring justice to her killer, and bless her family with the peace of closure…."

Lauren began, "Father, it's no coincidence that You have brought us here to Magnolia Falls at this time, with our old classmates. It's part of Your plan that we join forces to fight this enemy. You have blessed each of us with gifts to use to our fullest." Lauren paused, and Dee felt pressured to say something.

She hadn't prayed aloud in years.

The silence lengthened as Dee struggled to find the right words to say.

"Holy Father," Dee said quietly, "help me to accept that You are the ultimate judge and jury, that we are merely Your hands here on earth. Open my eyes and heart, Lord, to the ways that I can serve You…."

Edgar breathed a silent prayer, praising God for restoring Dee's faith in Him. He recalled Lauren's concern during college about her sister's struggle with her lost faith. He could feel joy fill the air.

"Amen," Lauren said before she threw her arms around Dee. Words weren't needed.

Dee's eyes looked tired and Edgar couldn't help

but wonder if she had truly been resting over the weekend. He hoped so, but it didn't seem to be the case.

It hadn't been easy to turn away from her just when they were becoming close. He admired her so much, it hurt to know that someone in their office was spreading damaging rumors about them. He hadn't wanted to tell Dee, but knew it would've only been worse if she heard it later from someone else.

"Did someone cut the wire?" she asked, bringing them back to the present.

"It doesn't look like it. It looks like the weight of the limb pulled it out of the connection to the house. You didn't hear the limb break?"

"No. It could have been before we got home, or for that matter, maybe that's what made Tipsy go crazy, and we just heard the crash of the vase." Dee headed out the garage door to the back of the house and found the limb that Edgar was talking about. "This is getting too coincidental, isn't it? Where'd I leave my cell phone? I'm going to call the phone company."

"Maybe you left it in your car Friday night," Edgar suggested.

Dee opened the door and, sure enough, there it was, on the console. She had eight missed calls. "Would you all like some coffee before we go?"

"No thanks. I hate to hurry everyone, but I have dinner plans with my future in-laws this afternoon," Steff said. "Trevor insisted they'd understand if I'm a little late. So, should I meet you at the fire department, or the police department?"

"According to the news, the fire department is running this investigation. We're the only ones who believe it's all connected somehow. I think we should talk to Jim Anderson or Nikki Rivers, since they're handling the investigations on the other cases. They at least know what we've been through."

"Steff brought her own car, so I'll ride with her and call the station to let them know we need to talk to someone," Lauren said. "Dee…"

"I'll take my car so no one has to bring me back out here later."

Before Dee knew it, the four of them were in the police department talking, yet again, to Detectives Anderson and Rivers.

"So what's happened now?" Detective Rivers asked, looking as if she was trying hard not to sound annoyed.

Lauren started out. "About a week ago, I saw a blog entry with a picture of the entire class at the reunion with flames burning in front of it. Computerized flames…"

"Yes, your sister told us about it. So, now, since there was a little fire behind Burt's, you think it was a warning?" Detective Anderson concluded. "You may not realize how often there are trash fires behind restaurants," he added.

"I received a phone call right before five o'clock," Dee began. Detective Anderson cleared his throat, and Dee said, "Excuse me, Detective, I know you think we're blowing this all out of proportion, but I'm as anxious to get rid of these threats as you are. Unfortunately, as the spokesman for the college, I'm in the limelight now. A woman called to tell me someone is posing as Josie on the Web site. Our call was cut off. I waited an hour for her to call back."

"Did you get a name?"

"I tried. She was—"

"A number?" Detective Anderson asked, interrupting her.

Detective Rivers held out her hand. "Wait a minute. Let her finish," she said. "How'd she know to reach you?"

"That's what I wondered at first. But she must have seen the press conference on TV."

"So," the female detective closed her eyes and concentrated. "Someone thinks Josie is missing…maybe this Josie is a possibility for our victim. So what else was said?"

"It sounded like she was on a cell phone because she kept breaking up. She said 'Mother and Father don't want me calling, but I know something is wrong.' Then someone yelled in the background. Then it got very quiet, muffled, like she was in a closed-in area. She said my name, then said I needed to find out who is pretending to be Josie, and we were disconnected. But that wasn't all."

The female officer became more interested. "And you don't have any idea who the caller was?"

"The voice sounded familiar, but I still can't place it exactly. She sounded very formal, using *Mother* and *Father* instead of more casual *Mom* and *Dad*…"

Detective Anderson was clearly annoyed. "Yeah, I get it. So do y'all have any idea who Josie is?"

"I thought she was referring to Josie Skerritt, a girl who went to school with us. Then, I went to the library at about seven o'clock to look at old yearbooks and see if some pictures of old classmates might bring to mind whose voice it was." Dee hesitated to tell them about the person in the black hooded sweatshirt.

She was sounding paranoid, even to herself. "When I walked from the administrative building to Kessler Library, I kept seeing someone in a black hooded sweatshirt following me and later, when I went inside, a small woman was standing outside the door with a black sweatshirt, but the hood wasn't up."

"You could tell it was a woman, but you can't describe her?"

"By then it was dark and I couldn't tell who it was."

Nikki Rivers furrowed her brow. "Then how could you tell it was a woman rather than a man?"

Dee closed her eyes and shrugged. "I guess I assumed it was a woman. She was rather petite and had a ponytail."

"How much later was that?" Anderson asked.

Dee looked at Edgar. "What time did you and Christiana see me?"

Edgar was pensive. He explained that they were so late because Christiana went to watch David Rutherford's basketball game. "Probably between eight and eight thirty."

"So it was at least an hour after I'd seen someone fitting the same general description follow me from building to building." Dee hurried through the story before they stopped her again. "Then Edgar and Christiana offered to take me to Burt's Pizza. We were there until close to ten."

"So were a lot of other people," Jim Anderson pointed out. "Listen, I know that when you're in the middle of an investigation, every little thing starts to look suspicious. We talked to the fire chief, and it looks like it was a smoldering cigarette that started the flames. Could have been anyone from an employee out on break to some drunk passing through the alley looking for free food."

"But it could have been a warning, too," Dee said, standing. She leaned forward, placing her hands on the table they were all crowded around. "My house has been vandalized twice, and my sister's been attacked." She looked at Steff, then back at the officers, tapping her finger on the officer's folder. "Our friend's brother was killed, Cassie Winters has been shot, and now that I'm the spokesperson for the college, you don't think it's more than a little coincidental that I'm getting threats?"

"Calm down, Miss Owens," Detective Rivers said sympathetically. "We're not saying we don't believe y'all. But we have to remain objective, look at this without bias." She jotted notes on a pad of paper, looked through a folder and glanced back up to the four of them, while Jim Anderson tapped his pencil on his notebook. "Whenever I go to a blog, it allows me to post anonymously. From what our computer geeks tell us, we can't locate anyone through a blog entry."

"I've suggested that we close the reunion Web site altogether," Edgar said, taking hold of Dee's hand. He tugged her toward him. "It's okay, Dee. Sit back down and let's talk it out."

"Actually," Detective Rivers said, "we have more leads from the Web site right now than anywhere else. The person who is sending the messages through it realizes he or she is able to voice these warnings anonymously without being traced." Nikki Rivers tucked a stray lock of hair behind her ear. "I realize it does create problems, but maybe we should have our techs find some way to change it to an e-mail user group without alerting anyone that it's being changed. We need some way to track the Internet address to a specific computer. Maybe there's something new out there that would work."

"Do I need to bring my laptop in to you?" Dee asked as she sat down, sending Edgar a smug look of satisfaction.

The female detective seemed to have taken charge. It was nice to finally receive serious consideration. "I'm not sure. I have your number, Miss Owens. I'll have someone from our investigations lab contact you. I've been a little concerned that we'd scare the suspect away by making the changes, but we do need to step things up if we're going to flush him or her out. We'll get some ideas from the IT guys and see what they may be able to set up with your site. For now, don't mention *any* changes to *anyone*. I'll have one of our investigators pose as an alumnus and monitor what's going on. They've been checking it out now and then, but apparently you removed the file before he saw it."

"So you do think these warnings have a tie to the murder?" Lauren asked in disbelief.

Jim Anderson nodded. "We never doubted it had something to do with something. It just wasn't fitting together how."

"Not that it is now," Nikki Rivers added. "But it's almost too coincidental that this is all coming to a head at the same time if it's not. Somehow, the skeleton, Scott's murder and the point-shaving must be connected. I just wish we could figure out how."

"What about the new evidence?" Edgar spoke up. "Have you found any clues there?"

"Getting closer," the middle-aged man said, rubbing his jaw. "That's as much as we can say right now. Unless you have something else, we'll be in touch..."

"Well, there might be one more coincidence," Edgar said. "I tried to call Dee yesterday, but she never answered. Today we went out to her house, and a tree limb appears to have knocked out her phone."

"We'll go check it out," Nikki Rivers said. "Have you called the phone company yet?"

"I was going to, but I want to be there when they come to look at it."

"Let us take a look first. We'll be out this afternoon, just in case someone tampered with it." Detective Rivers wrote down her address again and took Dee's cell phone number.

"We'll get back to you as soon as we have more information," Jim Anderson added. "And don't hesitate to call. We're as frustrated with the pace of the investigation as you are, but we always want to know if something happens. One of these days, this suspect is going to mess up."

Dee left the police station with renewed hope in the system and hoped her sister and friends felt similarly. As soon as they walked out the doors, Lauren's fiancé, Seth Chartrand, jumped out of his car and met them. His son waited in the backseat of the car.

"So? How'd it go?" Seth asked.

Lauren's focus had barely left Dee and Edgar since he'd told Dee to sit down. "Fine. I'm trying a new recipe for Sunday dinner. Would y'all like to join us at Seth's?"

Steff was the first to respond. "Thanks for the invite, but I'm late to meet Trevor's family. I'll talk to you tomorrow."

"Tell him hi," Lauren said with a smile. "And what about you two?"

Edgar blushed even through his dark skin. "I need to pick up Christiana from the skating rink at two-thirty. But thank you for the invitation." He backed away. "I'll see you at work tomorrow, Dee. Do be careful."

She watched him walk away, trying to tell herself that she didn't really care. Trouble was, she couldn't convince herself. Not even today, when she was still mad at him. "I'd love to come," Dee admitted. "We need to get busy planning the—"

"Don't try to change the subject, Deandra," her sister said. "What is going on with you two?"

"Absolutely nothing," Dee said calmly, determined to end this discussion now.

Seth hid a smile. "We'll see you at the house, Dee."

Dee had ten minutes to figure out how to avoid the topic of Edgar Ortiz.

TWELVE

Edgar hurried away from the police station and headed to the Half Joe for a quick bite, since Christiana and David would be eating at the skating rink with the youth group. He would have loved to have spent the afternoon with Dee, Lauren, Seth and his son, but he also had a lot of things to get organized for his recruiting trips this week.

Besides the fact that he'd hurt Dee's feelings by telling her about the rumors, he wasn't about to give her false expectations about his feelings. Sure he cared for her, but right now he was more concerned about protecting her. He was the reason she was being threatened, and he needed to stay focused on getting her out of the limelight.

He also needed to figure out how to approach the employee who'd started the indecent accusations about his relationship with Dee.

As he ate the hamburger and fries, his mind wandered back to the reunion when he'd finally met Dee Owens in person. The woman in the red dress had caught his eye immediately when she and her sister had walked into the Mossy Oak Inn.

Dee Owens. Lauren's older sister. He'd known Lauren from Campus Christian Fellowship, and knew who her outgoing sister was, but they hadn't been formally introduced. He'd admired Dee, one of the popular girls on campus, from afar, but even with the small campus, they'd never crossed paths. When he'd seen her at the reunion, mingling with classmates that he'd barely known, she'd taken his breath away.

At first he had been struck by her blond hair and blue eyes, always a killer combination for him. But it had been more than that, he realized now. He had suspected it was more than Dee's studies that kept her away from the Sunday night fellowship in college. He had wondered what had caused two sisters who had been raised in the same home to take such different paths. It had taken all the courage he'd possessed to approach Lauren with such personal questions.

He'd battled with his interest in Dee ever since that night, unable to turn away from his attraction, despite his suspicion that she wasn't a believer. He'd prayed for strength to resist her, but God seemed to have other plans. Instead of avoiding her, their paths kept crossing, and then the skeleton had been found, and he'd convinced the board that they needed to hire her.

Finally, hoping God would answer his prayers to dissolve his attraction to Dee, Edgar asked Lauren to join him for coffee at the Half Joe one morning a few weeks after the reunion. He'd been fully honest with Lauren. His conscience wouldn't allow him to dig into Dee's personal matters without divulging his intentions—he wanted to know Dee better.

Lauren hadn't given much information at first, overwhelmed by his honest approach. But it wasn't long before she opened up, even encouraging him to ask her sister out.

"Maybe after this scandal is over. It would be terribly awkward with her working in the same office," he'd admitted. "But after she's through at the college, it's a definite possibility, depending on what you can tell me."

"Dee's best friend died when they were twelve," Lauren had recalled. "I know that was when she changed, but I'm not one-hundred-percent sure why, and she won't talk about it. I tried to talk to her for a while, but it was for deeper issues than I could handle. I turned it over to God. She never criticizes my faith, so I don't think it's that she's denounced her belief, if that's why you're concerned. I think a lot of us could have walked away from our faith if God hadn't sent the right person to minister to our needs at the right time in our lives. I keep praying that in His time, she'll get past whatever happened."

Edgar paid for his meal, and as he drove to the skating ring to wait for his mind still reeled through what Lauren had said. Was Dee needing someone to minister to her and guide her? Was that why they had hit it off now? Was he the one God wanted to reach out to her?

That seemed forever ago, he thought. Before the

skeleton and the scandals had rocked the foundation of the college and the community.

He looked up and saw Christiana and David, then beeped the horn. He needed to get packed, make sure Christiana finished her report, and check his itinerary for the next recruiting fair. They were running out of time to repair the damage to their attendance numbers.

"Hi, Mr. Ortiz," David Rutherford said as he climbed into the car after Christiana.

"Hello, David," Edgar said as he waited for them to close the door and buckle up. "How was the skating party?"

"It was great. Can we go to a movie tonight?" Christiana asked.

He shook his head as he backed out of the parking space. "We have a lot to do this afternoon. I haven't seen you work on your report at all, and it's due tomorrow, isn't it?"

She groaned. "I can get it done. Come on, Edgar, it's the opening weekend."

"No Christiana." He looked in the rearview mirror, catching his rebellious sister as she formed a *W* with her hands. "I saw that."

"Good," she said, rolling her eyes.

"Yeah, it is good. I'm getting tired of you arguing with me all the time, Christiana."

"Whatever," she said sarcastically.

"It's okay, Christiana," David said quietly. "I'll find some way to get out of the house."

"I enjoyed watching your ball game Friday night, David."

"Thanks. I wish I'd have gotten to play more," he said. "But I guess it really isn't that big of a deal. I'm not going to be good enough to play college ball anyway."

"What makes you think that?" Edgar asked. "You're a junior, there's plenty of time to improve your game with summer camps and practice."

"My dad says I'm not built to play ball, so I'd better work on my grades if I want to go to college."

Edgar felt the anger stab him in the heart. "Grades are always number one in school, but that doesn't mean you should give up on your dream to play ball of any kind."

"Yeah, but if you're good enough, grades aren't that big of a deal. The school can help you pass your classes."

From anyone else, Edgar wouldn't have thought his comment was strange, but from a professor's child, it raised all sorts of flags.

"Did you play?" David asked.

"Yeah, I played soccer in Brazil," Edgar said, still distracted by David's comment. "I played until I came to America."

"Why'd you stop? We have soccer here."

"School was more important to me. By then, my father had died and my mother was ill. I knew I'd need to get my degree if I wanted to support myself and Christiana. I was also older when I went to college, so that was very different."

David looked at Christiana. "Is it hard not having your dad around?"

Christiana shrugged. "I was so little when he died, I don't know. It's all I've known, having a controlling brother running my life."

"I think you're pretty lucky to have a cool brother instead of a grumpy old man for a dad," David said somberly as Edgar pulled up to the Rutherford mansion.

Just as they stopped, a car pulled in behind them and Detectives Rivers and Anderson got out.

"Maybe I can call you tonight?" David asked.

Christiana shrugged. "It's fine with me, but you'd better ask the boss!"

Edgar looked at David and smiled. "You can give it a try, David. We'll have to see if the princess is out of solitary confinement by that time."

"Hello, Mr. Ortiz. Fancy meeting you here."

"Yes, it is, isn't it? Are you here to see me, or," he said hopefully, "someone else?"

"We came to talk to Rutherford, but we have a couple more questions for you. We went out to check out Miss Owens's tree and found a man's glove caught on the branch. Do you recall seeing it?"

"No," he said, puzzled.

"Do you own a pair of gloves?"

Edgar opened the console between the bucket seats and pulled out a pair of tan gloves. "Just these."

"Thanks, Edgar. That's all we need for now."

They rode home in silence, Edgar unable to get his mind off the peculiar comments that David had made about college sports. They could have only come from his dad, Professor Rutherford. If Christiana hadn't been in the car, he would have said something to the detectives about them.

Or did the police already know?

THIRTEEN

Dee rang the doorbell to Seth's house, still trying to come up with ways to avoid talking about her feelings for Edgar. She could ask why Lauren hadn't used the key to her house earlier that morning. She could also distract her sister with questions about the wedding. There were the investigations they could talk about, but she'd thought enough about those for the day.

"Hi, come on in," Seth greeted her. Dee was still working to forgive Seth for breaking up with her sister for another woman all those years ago. And now they were back together and engaged, in a matter of weeks.

"Hi Seth," she said, happy that the two were finally going to have the life together that they should have had from the beginning. She just wished Seth hadn't taken that little detour in life. Lauren's words echoed in her head. *I never stopped loving him. Seth realized he'd made a mistake, but not until she was pregnant. He honored his vows, and I can't help but respect him for that.* Dee had to hold on to the hope that God's plan was going to work out for them, even if it wasn't for her. "I see my sister's already starting to redecorate for you."

Seth laughed. "It needed a woman's touch."

"Better your house than mine, I guess."

He laughed again, harder this time.

"It wasn't that funny, Seth." Dee started laughing at the sound of his laugh. It was like a contagious yawn—as much as she wanted to avoid it, she couldn't.

"What's funny is that's what she said you'd say if she wanted to move her things into here before the wedding. You know her well."

Dee shrugged. "Sounds like it's Lauren who knows me." Somehow, that was going to come back at her, and probably before the day was over.

Despite Dee's reluctance to warm up to Seth and Jake, she was finding it hard not to. Lauren was happier than she'd seen her in years. "So, you two, when's this wedding taking place? Any hints yet?"

"As soon as things settle down," Lauren insisted.

"I wanted to get married next month, but your sister wants to wait until the case is solved, let everyone get back to normal first."

Dee looked at her sister. "So you're going to keep up this double life? Fixing dinner here and coming home to my place late at night? Now that makes no sense at all. And don't you dare tell me it's because you're worried about me. I have enough guilt as it is."

"And what do you have to feel guilty about?"

Lauren teased. "It wouldn't have anything to do with Edgar, would it?"

"Edgar?" Dee said with a laugh. "Nothing is going on with Edgar. I meant because of you being attacked at my house and your computer being stolen because of the Web site." Dee took a bite of the sugar snap peas that her sister had just pulled from the refrigerator.

"So then why did he blush when we asked him to come over for dinner?" Lauren teased as she seared the chicken and left it to simmer while she cleaned an assortment of vegetables.

Seth broke into the conversation. "Grown men don't blush, Lola."

Dee paused, stunned to hear Seth use the nickname he'd had for Lauren in high school. "See, Edgar wasn't blushing…"

"He was hot under the collar," Seth said with a coy smile.

"Which is about the same thing as the female version of blushing," Lauren argued.

"No, it's not," he countered.

"You say tomato, I say to-mah-to. Same thing." Lauren laughed, and Dee scowled at him.

She had to change the subject. "I wouldn't know. So are you ready for the moving truck yet?"

"He cares about you, Dee. I could see he was smitten at the reunion. He didn't leave your side. At church this morning it was obvious that he was worried sick about you."

Dee ignored her until she couldn't stand the

smugness on her sister's face. She wasn't about to let her get the last word in.

"You weren't even with me at the reunion. You and Jennifer went off and left me with Edgar. It just so happened that he was too polite to run off like you did."

"Because I could see that sparkle in his eye," she said with a lilt in her voice. "Besides, Jennifer wanted me to help her find something for the skit. It was you two who didn't see anyone else that night," she said, raising her eyebrows. She sidled up to Seth.

Her sister hadn't lost her sparring ability at all, probably from practicing debate with Seth as he was getting ready for a trial or something. Time to change the subject.

"The security system worked great, even through the thunderstorm. I peeked in on the carriage house this morning, it's just as you left it. No one is going to get into the house. And if they do, Tipsy is a great guard—" She stopped mid-sentence, realizing she was going to have to weasel her way out of telling them about what had happened Friday night.

"Edgar didn't date much in college, you know…" Lauren went on about what she'd found out from Steff during the drive out to her house that morning. "From what Steff said, he…"

Dee was determined to change the subject.

"It's just guilt again," Dee said. "Edgar is worried because he doesn't want to be responsible if I get hurt because of the job. It has nothing to do with me personally…"

"Stop it," Lauren snapped. "That's not how Edgar is. And I think you know that, too. This isn't because he got you the job at the college. You see each other about every day. Edgar cares about *you*. He came to me to see how you were today, Deandra!"

Dee thought for a few moments. "Then if he wants the rumors to stop, he'd better stop worrying and asking other people about me, hadn't he? It's obviously not just *my* eyes lighting up when I see him."

Lauren and Seth smiled at each other. "Rumors?"

Dee hesitated. "He says the women in the office at the college are talking about my success, and well, I presume they're saying we're…that I'm…not acting in a very professional…"

Their smiles disappeared. "They didn't! About Edgar? He's their boss! They should know him better than to think that."

Dee's jaw dropped. "It's okay if they say it about me, though? With a sister like this, who needs enemies!"

Lauren turned red, and Seth smiled as he teased Lauren. "That's definitely a tomato."

Lauren brushed him aside. "Of course I didn't mean it that way, Dee, but they don't know you. Yes, it's wrong for them to look at your success and make a judgment. But think about how it would feel to be Edgar. They've worked with him for years, and they should know he isn't that kind of man."

Dee couldn't believe she'd actually told them. "I've never dated a coworker, let alone a boss. I don't even want to finish out the job. I don't want anyone thinking that about either of us, but I shouldn't have to…" She closed her eyes and felt her emotions creeping up on her. It wasn't just the rumors. She couldn't stand the thought of not seeing Edgar again.

"Don't do that, Dee. Edgar will set them straight and deal with their gossiping. I know that kind of behavior won't be tolerated," Seth assured her. "As much as we've unmercifully teased you, I hope you know we don't mean it in the way the gossips do." It touched Dee that Seth was able to joke around and also defend not only Lauren, but her family, too. "Lauren and I want you to find someone special like we have. I've known Edgar a long time, and I can't help but be biased. He'd make a great brother-in-law."

Dee's jaw dropped. "What?"

"You heard me," Seth replied. "And I mean it."

"There's something major missing first. Every time I think he's interested, he backs away. I need to figure out why I wouldn't make a great wife."

Dee watched as Lauren tossed the vegetables into the hot skillet and let them sizzle. Seth planted a kiss on Lauren's lips and smiled. "I'm going to go get Jake."

Lauren watched silently as her fiancé walked down the hall. "I don't think I could have apologized any better myself. Seth isn't just trying to win you over, Dee. He wants you to be happy, too."

Dee rolled her eyes with a smile. "Yeah, he's a good guy, but I still think he's trying to win me over. And yes, it's working. For your happiness, I'd forgive just about anyone anything."

"Uh-huh. And now you know why I'm not going to let him get away a second time. He's trying to convince me to have a small wedding next month, just a few friends and family. I'm also going to make a recommendation, Dee, and I want you to think about it, seriously."

"What's that? Get married so you don't have to stay at my house and pretend to be my roommate?" Dee smiled.

"Almost," Lauren said, lightening the mood again as she moved the rice from the pan to a platter. "Seth suggested you and I move into the extra bedrooms here until these threats are over. I know you've installed—"

"Thanks for the offer, but..." She realized she was doing it again, pushing away people who were trying to help her. She needed to drop her guard, test the waters of giving up control. "I'll have to think about it. And you know Mom and Dad will never stand for you two moving in together."

"That isn't it at all, Dee. We're waiting until we're married. This really is about our safety. Even if the security system does alert the police, it could take far longer for them to get to your house than it would for someone to hurt us. I'll only make the move here if you'll come, too. Temporarily, just until this stalker is caught. And if that happens, we'd move the wedding plans up a little," Lauren said.

Dee started searching for the dishes, opening and closing each cabinet one at a time. "You're too nice to say you won't get married because you feel like you need to watch out for me, Lauren. But if you're waiting on me to find Mr. Right before you'll get married, you're going to die an old maid."

Lauren smiled with a seriousness that was almost frightening. "Don't worry, I'm not waiting any longer than I need to. I know it sounds odd to say this, but I was absolutely sure four months ago that Seth and I would never see eye to eye again. I was sure that I'd never find Mr. Right. God knows when our hearts are ready. And when the time is perfect, God will have the right man fall head over heels in love with you. He'll give everything up to be with you, it's going to be so right."

"Mr. Right is an illusion. I don't think I'm the marrying kind."

Seth walked past and went to the only cabinet that she hadn't looked in. He started setting the table. "Oh, yeah? And what kind are you?"

She took a bite of a carrot stick and asked where to find the silverware. "The career woman, I guess. I think maybe I'm too intimidating."

Jake chose that moment to enter the kitchen. "What is that?" Jake asked.

"What's what, Jake?" Dee asked, ready for a distraction. She had to admit, it was fun to have kids around again. Her folks were already enjoying being grandparents.

"Endmitating," he said awkwardly.

Dee smiled. "In-tim-i-dating," she said slowly. "It means frightening."

"Jake, does Aunt Dee scare you?" Lauren asked.

He thought a minute, then nodded emphatically. "Yeah, sometimes, when we play space cowboys."

Dee laughed. "Wait a minute, I was the princess."

"Yeah, the princess always was pretty bossy," Seth said with another ornery laugh.

"Bossy?" Dee laughed. "Yeah, well, I suppose I do qualify for that one." She set down the rest of the silverware. "Jake, how about if you help me set the silverware on the table?"

"I do that all the time. Don't you have your Palm here that I could play games on?"

"Actually, the battery is low, so I need to charge it up. Maybe next time," she whispered.

"It's time to eat anyway, Jake." Lauren put the finishing touches on the dish and pulled some nongluten flatbread from the cupboard for Jake and a loaf of French bread for the rest of them.

They bowed their heads to bless the food, and Dee felt different afterward. Maybe it was left over from the morning, or maybe it was a continuation. Whatever the reason, it felt right, and she wanted to find a way to make it last.

An hour later, they'd started to talk about wedding ideas when she received a call from Detective Rivers. "Dee, we're out at your house."

She felt a chill run up her spine. "Hi, Detective. Did you find something else?"

"As a matter of fact, yes, we did. A black leather glove in the middle of the branch that fell on the wire."

"No! Not again..." Dee turned to Lauren and Seth.

"Could either of you have dropped a black leather glove?"

"Dee," Nikki said, to get her attention again. "Dee…" she yelled.

Dee put her finger to her mouth to quiet them. "Yes?"

"It's a man's glove. A *very* nice glove, kid leather. Who has been in your backyard recently?"

Dee looked at Seth and Lauren. "Well, Edgar… Ortiz went out to check the phone line this morning. And Seth Chartrand was last out there to get my sister's bags to go to Savannah, on Friday afternoon, I believe. Just a minute."

Seth had already gone to the closet and returned with a matched pair of gloves. "I don't have black gloves, but my brown pair is here. I haven't worn them at all this winter. I've never seen Edgar wear gloves, either, but I can call him if you'd like."

"Dee, tell Mr. Chartrand we've already spoken to Mr. Ortiz," Nikki responded, and Dee was angry that he'd found out about it before she had. Then she had a sudden chill at the thought that again, someone had been outside her house, within feet of the back door. Edgar had been there, but surely the police weren't going to treat him like a suspect.

"Dee, are you okay?" Detective Rivers asked.

"Well, sort of. I don't know. Are you saying the fallen branch and the downed line wasn't caused by the storm?"

It was quiet far too long. "We aren't going to be able to say for sure. The line doesn't look at all like it was cut. But the branch fell off the tree trunk several feet away. We can see a divot where the branch landed. There are no marks on the wire, so it doesn't really look like it was hit by the branch."

"And the glove was underneath the branch?"

"Actually, it was caught on it. That's the odd thing. It was caught in a place that doesn't seem logical if someone was wearing the glove when they moved the branch. And there are some muddy footprints, but with the heavy rains, we won't be able to tell much from that, either. We'll talk with some of your neighbors, see if they've seen or heard anything the last few days. Could you confirm with Lauren that the branch wasn't down when they left on Friday?"

Dee was numb, but she managed to ask.

Lauren took the phone. "No, the yard was clean when we left," she answered. "I picked Jake up from school at three and we went to Seth's house until he was off work. We stopped by Dee's house between six and six-thirty, just long enough to pick up my bag."

Lauren handed the phone to Dee.

"Dee, we've collected all the evidence we could gather," Detective Rivers said. "So you can call the phone company to get it connected again. We're going to take the branch and see what our lab can figure out. Would you ask the repairmen to call us if they find anything else out of the ordinary?"

"Sure." Out of the ordinary? What exactly was ordinary? She couldn't even remember those days. When would her life be ordinary again?

FOURTEEN

Dee arrived at the college early Monday morning, hoping to finish her work and get to Savannah before Edgar realized she'd even been there. She didn't know how he felt about the police questioning him, but she wasn't sure she could deal with Edgar's reaction right now anyway. She needed him to take a look at the lists she and Steff had prepared Friday afternoon. If he approved the letter, they could have them out by the end of the day.

The only motivation she had for being in the office right now was to help Edgar keep their numbers from falling any lower. She had to prove to anyone questioning her skills that she deserved to be there. She studied the data from previous years and looked at the falling trend for the current year. It didn't look promising, but if they handled things right, they could change it.

"Dee Owens." A low voice came from her doorway.

She looked up from the computer screen and was

sickened to see Cornell Rutherford. There weren't too many people that Dee could honestly say she really didn't like. He was one of them.

"You're a busy lady these days." Cornell Rutherford said with a smile that turned her blood cold.

She considered herself fortunate that she'd made it through four years of college without ever having to have even one personal conversation with the man. "Good morning, Dr. Rutherford. Are you looking for someone?"

"You," he said. "I want to talk to you about representing the college. It seems highly inappropriate, under the circumstances."

There was something very uncomfortable about his presence. "I'm afraid I don't know what circumstances you're referring to. What seems to be the problem?"

His full-length leather overcoat flowed like silk with his every move. "It appears as if there's a conflict of interest that we may need to discuss with the board of trustees, Miss Owens. A matter of personal judgment, I'm sure, but I would hate to see anything else rock the foundation of the college. I think the games you're all playing on the Web site have gone on long enough. It's making the entire college look corrupt and I'm sure the board will agree, even if Edgar doesn't. And I believe it's highly inappropriate that you're *more* than a little involved with *both*."

There was nothing cordial in his tone, which caught Dee off guard. She didn't know how to respond. Was Rutherford implying that she and Edgar were involved? Or did he mean "both" to be the Web site and the college?

"I appreciate you sharing your concerns, Cornell," Edgar said as he entered Dee's office, briefcase still in his hand.

Cornell spun around to see Edgar. He jutted out his chin. Dee noticed a deep cut on his jaw underneath the clear bandage. It was also just beyond his goatee, but it looked too wide a gash to be a shaving nick. "Edgar, I'm surprised to see you here so early."

"I wasn't aware that you kept track of my hours, Cornell."

Dr. Rutherford was too startled by the confrontation to object.

Edgar went on. "Ms. Owens and I have discussed the Web site with powers-that-be and decided that it will stay. Any further discussion should be taken to the board."

Edgar's broad shoulders seemed to fill the room as he defended the Web site, and Dee's heart swelled with affection. She knew how difficult it was for Edgar to leave the Web site active—let alone defend it.

"You shouldn't be taking any chances either, Edgar. Enrollment has hit rock bottom, and that isn't going to look good when the board reviews your application for Director of Admissions. Don't get too comfortable in this interim position."

His application? The board had made the decision to move him to interim director? Why hadn't Edgar told her he'd put his name in? Dee forced herself to keep a confident smile on her face, not let Cornell Rutherford see that he'd surprised her with the news. Edgar was here defending her, and the least she could do was stand by him and present a united front.

"News travels fast in the Kessler family, apparently."

"Yes," Cornell responded with an edge of discomfort.

How recent was this news? She recalled Friday night, wanting him to kiss her good-night and the disappointment when he'd insisted they had to keep their distance. This was why. It was beginning to make sense now. But why hadn't Edgar told her? Though it wouldn't have made it much easier to curb her feelings, it would have helped.

Edgar didn't waver. "It's difficult to turn down a request to submit an application when it comes from the board of trustees. Still, I'm not concerned about anything they might want to know about me, or what they'll find. If it's meant to be, it will happen. David played a very good basketball game Friday night, by the way. It's too bad you missed it."

Dr. Rutherford glared at Edgar, then back to Dee. "I'd be very careful with that ridiculous Web site. If one more allegation shows up about me, I'm going to be filing charges against you two personally!" Standing ramrod straight, Cornell charged out of the office.

Dee moved to close the door. Then she remembered the gossips who would have a heyday if they were in here together and left it open. Hopefully, the culprits weren't in yet. "I didn't like him before, and I like him even less now. That is one troubled man. Surely he can't believe he stands a chance of being named the next president of the college. And I hope the board has better sense than to consider him." She didn't want to seem possessive by mentioning Edgar's hopeful job change, but she was sure he'd know how much it hurt her to find out the news from Cornell Rutherford. At least, she hoped he did.

Edgar set his briefcase on the floor next to her desk, removed his overcoat, then pulled the chair closer to her and sat down. "I meant what I said to him, Dee. I've done nothing to be ashamed of. In the past, or the present. We may be working together, but I'm not your supervisor." Edgar's gaze darted to hers, then to the door. He seemed to want to say something else.

"I understand the complications now, Edgar. I've never believed in getting too close to a coworker, male or female. I've never been in this situation before, where I'm the one who wants to break my own rules," she said softly.

"No, it's not easy to eat your own words, is it? I meant to tell you about the application Friday, but everything went on another course than the one I anticipated. Let Rutherford take it to the board. If they feel I've acted inappropriately, I guess God has been trying to tell me it's time to move on after all."

His eyes clung to hers, analyzing her reaction.

He'd been practically obsessed with the effect the scandals would have on the college a few months ago. He'd pushed her to take this job. Pushed her for results. Surely he wasn't giving up now.

Or was he really backing away from her? Was she too assertive? Too stubborn? Too tied to her career?

She didn't dare push for answers now. She'd learned long ago not to ask a question unless she knew the answer. Right now, she not only didn't know the answers, she didn't know if she could deal with the answers if she had them. If they were meant to be, they would make it through this. She felt a sudden chill in the room. "Do you think he meant you and me when he mentioned my involvement with both?" She shook her head. "How would he even know? It was just barely Friday night that you even came close to kissing me."

"I have no doubt he meant us. With the rumors that have been flying around here, I wouldn't be too surprised if they made it across campus. Apparently our feelings regarding each other are worn on our faces," he said with a smile, "or however that saying goes."

Dee laughed, and it felt good to see that Edgar was nothing like the men she usually dated. Not many of them knew they had weaknesses. "I'm sorry about that, Edgar. I was beginning to think my own guilty conscience planted the innuendo in Rutherford's mind, that maybe he was just bluffing. He's definitely the type to think that he knows everything about everything."

Edgar shrugged. "You have nothing to feel guilty about. Maybe Christiana has mentioned you to David, but considering nothing has happened except a quick kiss, and she doesn't know anything about that, it can only be speculation. Even *if* someone did see us—" they could hear footsteps in the hallway "—that isn't a crime," he said vaguely.

"Regarding the Web site, we have to address this, one way or another." While he talked, Edgar glanced outside her office, then took out a pad of paper and scribbled a note to her. *Not a word to ANYONE about Rivers and Anderson's involvement! The board wants this solved at any expense. J.T. knows, and he's with us.*

Dee nodded. "Okay," she said hesitantly, hoping he didn't honestly think she would let that slip. She was the one fighting to keep the Web site up and running.

Without missing a beat, Edgar kept talking, keeping his voice low. "If this person keeps going on about Cornell, I wouldn't blame him for being upset. Whether the accusations are true or not, the damage would be done as far as public opinion goes. It's a liability to the college to have a loose cannon out there. You know how I feel about the link being on the official college Web site, Dee."

"I know." She looked up, reading the conflict in his expression. He was struggling with the police's request to keep it as it was.

"You have access to my calendar, right?"

His calendar? What was he changing the subject for? "I don't know—do I?"

"I think I set it up last week so you can look at it from your computer. Open your e-mail." He stood behind her and gave her instructions on how to access his calendar. "I'd like you to set up a meeting with Steff Kessler and the college legal counsel."

"Oh, yes, I have a new idea to run past you."

"My schedule is getting extremely tight, but this can't wait. The items in blue are flexible, those in red are not. See what works for everyone's schedules and we'll see where we stand."

Dee scribbled notes to herself. *Blue-flex, red-sis.*

He leaned closer to look at her writing. "Sis? What did I say?"

"You said they're not flexible, which I term 'set-in-stone'."

Edgar laughed. "I see."

"Edgar, I would like someone who isn't employed by the college to take over as Webmaster. I don't want Professor Rutherford to think he bullied us into submission, but then again, I need to focus on the school right now. I thought of asking Lauren if she would do it again, though with the wedding plans and starting her new catering business she's not able to keep an eye on it all the time either. I really think it's time we let the police take it over."

"He's really frightened you, hasn't he?"

She nodded. "I just can't shake the feeling that he's acting pretty guilty about something," she whispered again.

He stood and picked up his briefcase. "Do you have time later this morning for coffee?" he asked, suddenly in a hurry to leave.

"Sure, why?"

"There are a few other things I'd like to talk to you about. I'm headed to the high school to talk to my sister right now, but I'll call to schedule a place and time later, if that's okay."

His sudden commitment seemed to come out of nowhere. "Sure, I'll talk to you later, then," she said, puzzled by his cryptic comment.

What was he up to now?

FIFTEEN

"I've pushed as much as I dare without bringing more attention to myself. I told you to stop sending those e-mails."

"And I told you to get rid of Dee. She's getting too much information."

"We must have a bad connection. I thought you said Dee knows too much. Dee doesn't know anything!" he said adamantly. "She's scared speechless. Edgar came to her rescue, but I reminded him that he has a lot at stake now, too."

"Sticks and stones, Professor, words aren't enough! You should know that better than anyone, Professor. What was it you used to tell me in those private tutoring sessions?"

The caller let the silent threat speak for itself. His wife had never once suspected he'd strayed. He couldn't afford to let her find out now. It was her family name that kept him in the running for president.

"I want another payment to keep your little secret.

Of course, she's getting to be a bigger secret, and one of these days she's going to want to know who her daddy is…"

"Don't threaten me again. We had an agreement. Don't you dare back down on it now. You may have already blown it with your e-mails. I can't move any money right now or it will raise more questions, and then your little secret will be out as well."

She's not going to give up, he thought. If I could just find her, I could take care of everything. I've got to do something to keep her silent.

"Let's meet, and I'll bring you a partial payment…"

The line went dead.

SIXTEEN

Dee was still waiting on Edgar's call when Jameson King's name came up on the phone's caller ID an hour later. "Magnolia—" she answered, only to be cut off.

"Dee, it's Cassie."

She smiled. Cassie never did like to mince her words on formalities. "How are you feeling?"

"Better," Cassie replied. "I'm still working half days until my energy is full force again. I called to see if you can meet some of the girls and me for lunch today."

She looked at her watch and wondered when Edgar would want to meet. "I need to meet Edgar Ortiz sometime this morning, too. What time and where will you be? I'll try to make it if I can."

"Actually, Lauren offered to cook, and we agreed to try a new recipe for her. We're going to meet at Seth's at one. Kate's off today, so she's going to join us, and I'm still trying to convince Jennifer to come.

We've all been through so much lately that I felt we needed a break."

"That's the truth. We have a *lot* to share—I just hope one lunch hour is enough to get it all in! I'll see you later."

As soon as Dee hung up the phone, it rang again. Edgar wanted her to meet him in fifteen minutes at the Half Joe.

"Sure, that works perfect. I'll see you in a few minutes," Dee answered.

She grabbed the rough draft of the letter to get his approval on, and headed out the door.

Edgar had been waiting forty minutes and was getting worried. Dee had said she was leaving right after they'd hung up. He'd called her office again, but she'd left more than half an hour ago. Maybe they had mixed up where they were going to meet. He called her cell, but it went straight to voice mail, sending a chill up his spine.

The waitress stopped by again, and he hated to put her off much longer. Maybe he should go look for Dee. "Are you Edgar Ortiz?" the waitress asked.

"Yes. Why?"

"Dee Owens just called. She's been in a fender-bender and will be here as soon as they have the accident cleaned up."

He had a knot in his stomach. "Did she give you a location or a phone number?"

"Just that she's going to have the police drop her off here when they've finished."

Edgar waited impatiently, jumping to his feet when she walked in the door a few minutes later. "Dee, are you okay?" He rested his hand on her shoulder. "What happened?"

She nodded, her eyes revealing more than her words. "I'm okay, just mad."

"You're not hurt?"

She shook her head.

"Thank God. What happened?" Edgar led her to the booth near the entrance where he had been seated.

"I was crossing Peach Grove Lane at Tenth Avenue, and someone hit the back bumper of my car and spun me into oncoming traffic. They didn't even stop. The police had to call in a tow truck for my car. Could you give me a ride over to Seth's house after this, or should I see if Cassie can take me?"

"I'm afraid I need to head out to another high school after this. And I was hoping we could go to the police station, too. If Cassie can pick you up, that would be great." He closed his eyes slightly, wondering how she really felt. Did she honestly believe this was nothing more than an accident? "You have no idea who it was that hit you?"

"Not a clue. The car hit me from the rear, and it happened so fast, I didn't even see anything but a black streak when I spun around. What are you going to talk to the police about?"

"I'll explain in a minute. You make arrangements with Cassie first." She pulled out her phone and made a quick call to ask Cassie to pick her up on her way to lunch.

He waited impatiently until she'd finished her call. "Dee, this is getting dangerous."

Just then, the waitress stopped by to take their order. Dee had only a coffee since she was going to lunch with the girls, and Edgar ordered a sandwich.

"An auto accident isn't out of the ordinary, as the police reminded me. It could have happened to anybody sitting at that light. I don't normally leave the office for lunch. Surely no one has that much time on their hands to sit and wait for me to come and go. And if they do, well, I hope my schedule is driving them as crazy as it is me! Anyway, I'm okay now." Her full lips formed a straight line, no smile of reassurance.

She wasn't okay. Her blue eyes didn't look as bright and happy as they usually did when they were together. Of course, he'd handled everything wrong on Friday night. Unfortunately he didn't have time now to straighten that out. He looked at her as she pulled a paper from her briefcase. "What's that?"

Dee handed it to Edgar. "I brought the letter that Steff and I drafted for the alumni endorsements. If you can give me your approval, we'll get it out right away. And what—"

"May I take it with me and call you about it tonight? There are a few other things I wanted to talk to you about now." Edgar glanced at it, then set it aside.

"Sure," she said with questioning eyes. "What's up?"

Edgar's gaze met hers. "I think you're right about—" he lowered his voice "—Cornell."

Her eyes told him everything she felt. Fear, mingled with relief. "Oh Edgar, thank you. I thought…" She was near tears. "I hardly trust myself to think these days. I can't tell you how relieved I was that you stopped in the office when you did this morning. Was that what convinced you?"

"Partially."

Dee glanced around the café, then spoke softly, "Did you see the quality of his coat? Nice, like kid leather maybe?"

"Like the glove? I hadn't even thought of that," he muttered, apparently as concerned as she about being listened to. "Were any of your shades open Friday night, Dee?"

"No, not since Lauren's attack. One night we looked out after hearing something and I was just sure I'd seen someone in the trees across the street. Pretty soon, one of what I thought was a tree trunk ran down the street. I can't take that anymore, so we keep them closed all the time now."

The waitress brought their food and coffee, looking at them as if they were guilty of something.

As soon as the waitress was gone, they returned to their conversation. "I didn't remember them being open. I'm still trying to make sense of his comments this morning. I went to the school after I left the office and talked to Christiana. She and David haven't talked at all about you and me. Christiana seemed very happy to hear I've shown an interest in you."

Dee was deep in thought and missed his comment. "Well, what if he was driving by as we arrived? Never mind, I'm not exactly in the neighborhood for passersby. But since David and Christiana are seeing each other, I'm assuming he would recognize your car."

"True. I dropped David off yesterday afternoon. In fact, that's where I ran into the police." Edgar rubbed his hand through his hair. "They'd gone to question Cornell about something, I'm assuming. The odd thing was, David got out and saw the police, and you could see the fear plain as day on his face, but he didn't look surprised."

They were both silent for a few minutes as some faculty members walked into the cafe. "Even if it was *him* at my house Friday night, I can't understand why he'd risk coming into my office today. Could he really think we're not putting all of this together?" Dee took a long drink of her coffee.

"Maybe he simply saw us together at Burt's and jumped to the conclusion that we're seeing each other. That's right off campus, so that makes more sense. I keep trying to convince myself that these coincidences don't necessarily mean he's a stalker." He saw the disbelief in her eyes. "I know, I'm working through what I think the police will say if we try to tell them this."

"Well, his visit this morning was…creepy. The other day I was thinking about why I've never liked him. When we were in college, he had an affair with one of my dorm mates," she said, thinking about that scratch on his face. "Maybe that's who, or what the anonymous e-mail is referring to."

"Yeah, could be. We need to take every little detail into consideration, but it's so difficult to understand why he'd do this. When I picked up Christiana and David yesterday from the skating rink, David said some very strange things, too. He mentioned that his father advised him to give up on basketball and concentrate on his grades."

"That's kind of understandable. He is a professor."

"Yes, however," he said, speaking faster with each word, "David also said if you're a good athlete, grades don't matter, that the school will help make sure the good players pass their classes."

Dee's eyebrows arched high. "Edgar," she said as if that were the worst possible thing in the world. Dee glanced around the room and moved closer to Edgar. "Reese, the woman who was watching Jake and tried to scare away Lauren, was one of Rutherford's students. Maybe he's been using her."

Edgar shook his head. "I don't know what to think, but putting it all together, it's not looking good. I've an appointment to talk to Detective Rivers this afternoon, mention what David said, though I'd be shocked if they would involve his son at this point."

"Probably not. But I also plan to talk to them about Reese again. Maybe she'd come up with more information if she thinks the professor might be held accountable."

Edgar wondered why she'd started talking so nonspecific when he turned and noticed another English professor walk into the coffee house.

"Thanks, Dee. I don't mean to make this a battle, honest. It's just that it is going to impact the recruiting," he said, abruptly changing the subject. Holding the paper that Dee'd brought out in front of him, he nodded and smiled at another English professor who passed by their table. After he'd gone, Edgar returned to their discussion about Cornell. "And besides that, I have to keep peace with the man off campus, too. Christiana is still crazy about his son. David's a good kid, and I'd hate to see him dragged through the mud because of his father. They were having problems before those messages were released, and it's worse now."

Dee smiled. "Well, he couldn't have found a better man to look up to than you, Edgar. His own father has, at the very least, been less than a good example for years."

Dee watched as Edgar's face flushed to match his pink shirt. "I didn't say he was looking up to me, exactly. I will admit that David's been trying to spend more time away from his house. Last night when the police stayed at the car to ask me about the glove, David had a look of relief on his face. I'll never forget how quickly it changed from fear to relief."

"Relief?"

He nodded. "After we went home, Christiana finally confided in me that the police have questioned David's father."

Dee felt a heaviness lift from her shoulders. "I feel so much better, just knowing they've at least talked to him. Did she know when it was? Why?"

The contentment on Edgar's face was priceless, his smile as intimate as a kiss. "You went into PR because you like to be on the inside looking out, don't you? You love knowing things others don't."

Dee felt her skin turn warm. "I'd say it's more like not liking to be left in the dark. I'm much more content keeping a secret than having it kept from me." She smiled back, wondering if he'd understand her underlying message. As long as she knew he cared for her, she was fine. She only got upset when she didn't know how he felt.

"Point taken. I'll work on that one."

"So, did Christiana mention when or why?"

"She didn't know what about, just that David thought his dad was going to jail. So maybe seeing me get questioned made David think it wasn't such a big deal."

"Maybe, but I hope he isn't disappointed. Can you imagine how that would shake a teenager up?" She noticed Edgar nod. "I thought you were going to be gone today, though I'm very grateful that you were here to talk to Cornell."

"I was. I went in to get the newest brochures and pick up a college car. That, and I had a thought last night. The week after next week is our largest application fair. I hoped I could talk you into coming with me to speak. It's Tuesday evening, in Charleston, and, the next day, there are another two nearby, if you'd be interested in going."

"Actually, I was going over the data from the last few years, trying to come up with something new we could do to show Magnolia College's success stories. I was surprised to see the decline has been going on for a few years. The previous director shouldn't have waited until the scandal to do something."

"Yes, I suspect that has something to do with why he was asked to step down. Now it's my headache, as we like to say in Brazil."

Dee smiled. "Why not have some alumni go with us, well-known alumni. Like maybe Parker Buchanan. Every kid wants to be a comic book writer now."

"Why not you? You've made quite an impression on Christiana."

She looked into his brilliant brown eyes and smiled. "People around here may know me, but I'm far from famous."

"It's pretty short notice. We don't have much time to pull it all together, and the budget is going to be tight. Since you and Parker are local, let's keep it to you two this spring. By the time these letters come back, maybe we'll be able to get more interest for fall recruiting, if the school lasts that long."

She pulled her planner from her bag and opened it to that date. She had a couple of appointments that she'd need to reschedule, but the chance to be with Edgar would be worth it. "I'll e-mail you after I confirm my schedule. And after I convince Parker that we need him, too. We're not going to let Magnolia College be ruined by some sicko."

The smile on his face would definitely make rescheduling worth it. "That's a deal. Have I mentioned how impressed I am that you never let this get you down?"

"Thanks." She could almost withstand this if it wasn't having such a negative effect on her personal life. "Steff and I are going to mail out the first of the letters, unless you have any changes. Even if we can't take more to the recruiting fair, we have dozens of other alumni who have made great strides. How about if we add a paragraph to the letter about allowing us to feature them on our Web site?" She held up her hands like a movie director. "Right up there on the front page, no hiding them in the back of the alumni pages."

Edgar smiled. "I like that, too. What other ideas do you have tucked away?"

The check arrived, and Edgar left a bill to cover it. "Thank you for your patience, miss."

The waitress smiled.

"Will Cassie be here soon? I don't want to leave you alone."

She glanced at her watch and nodded, touched again by Edgar's chivalry. She was having a tough time getting used to that. Something told her it would be worth the effort, though. "Soon enough. I'll walk you to your car."

He held the door for her. "So, any other ideas?"

"Short term, I'm running pretty low, honestly. If the police were closer to making an arrest on the murder, we'd be much further ahead. We can't erase what's happened, but we can show that the college staff is doing everything possible to make sure it doesn't happen again."

Dee's phone rang and she dug through her purse to retrieve it, missing the call. "I hope Cassie isn't having car problems too. She's been driving her brother's old Mustang since he died."

"A red one? Nice ride."

She turned in the other direction. "That's her." Dee smiled at Edgar. "Have a good day, Edgar."

"You too. And be careful. I'll check in with you later." His smile erased the distance between them.

As Cassie pulled to a stop, Dee pulled her phone from her purse to see who'd called. Nikki Rivers.

What now?

SEVENTEEN

Dee opened the door and slid into the leather seat. "Hey there, Cass. It's so good to see you!" She leaned across the seat and gave her friend a hug.

"You too, Lauren has been telling me what's happened to you. This is just horrible. I thought about all we've been through and couldn't wait any longer for all of us to catch up with each other!" Cassie's red hair bounced. "So what happened to your car?"

"More bad luck, apparently." Dee told her about the accident.

"Kinda makes you want to just take a long vacation, doesn't it? And never come back," Cassie said with a smile. "Well, we have a lot to discuss today, then. I found my brother's notes and I need some help deciding where to start with them."

"You what?" Dee exclaimed. "You start by taking them to the police, of course."

"I know, I will. But I wanted all of you to look through them with me, see if we can make some sense of them first. I made copies and mailed them to the police and my lawyer, just in case something happens to the original."

A few minutes later, they were at Seth's house, greeting everyone. "Jennifer, Kate, it's good to see you!" Cassie's voice was bubbly. "Before we get down to the nasty news, I have some good news for y'all." She held up her hand and revealed an engagement ring.

"Cassie, and you brought us all here thinking this was just an ordinary lunch! I'd have made something really special if I'd known!" Lauren said. "Goodness, love seems to be the only thing getting any of us through lately, doesn't it?"

Dee watched with envy as her friends celebrated. She didn't want to put a damper on the party, but she did want to see this notebook.

"I just had to throw that out there to cheer everyone up before I showed you this." Cassie pulled the notebook from her purse. "It's Scott's notes on the stories he was writing. I found it under the floor mat in his car this morning as I was cleaning it out."

Kate's smile disappeared. "That's kind of a bittersweet gift, isn't it? Do you think it will be of any help?"

Cassie nodded. "Lauren, do we have a minute for me to show this to everyone before we eat?"

Dee's phone rang again. She looked, not surprised to see the detective's name.

She told the girls who it was, then answered.

"Hi Dee, it's Nikki Rivers."

"Hi Nikki. We're getting to be old friends."

"I heard about your accident. Are you feeling okay?"

"I'm a little sore, but otherwise, I'm fine."

Dee felt a tap on her shoulder. Cassie pointed to the notebook and whispered, "If that's the detective, ask her to come by now."

"Good. I'm beginning to be convinced that someone has it in for you. Good thing you have a guardian angel watching over you," said the detective.

That gave Dee pause. "Me, too."

"Dee, I'm calling because I think we have a possible identity of the person sending the e-mails."

"Who?" she blurted out.

"Daisy," she said hopefully. "Does that name ring a bell to you?"

Dee felt her hope take a nosedive. "No."

"Well, it looks like that's her online user ID. Very few people choose an ID that's similar to their real name. The techies were also able to get an Internet service provider number. They're going to run it through the state system and hopefully have a name soon."

"Really?"

"We're hoping," Nikki said. "I'll let you know if we find anything. And just for your information, we have definite initials on the charm. It's P.B. for sure."

"Wow, that's great! And we have more news to share with you, also. Cassie Winters is here at Seth's house. She found her brother's notebook. Can you come by?"

"We'll be right there."

Dee got off the phone and looked at the wide eyes of her friends. "She's on her way."

"And?" Steff asked. "What did she call for?"

"She thinks they have a lead on the person sending the e-mails. Does Daisy bring anyone to mind for any of you?"

"No," Lauren said. "I don't think I've seen that name. So, Cassie, before the detectives come and take the book, let's take a quick peek. Any hints of who might have come after Scott?"

"He has a lot of names. I recognize a few of them. Most were basketball players."

Dee shared the information Edgar had heard from David Rutherford. "And of course, he's telling the police, but please don't say anything outside of these walls. We've all had enough trouble without someone out there thinking we know something they don't want us to."

"Did you look into any of the names in the school records? Maybe the police can find someone else that knew this was going on?" Steff asked.

"No," Cassie said. "I'm like Dee, I don't want to let anyone know we've found this. I made a copy and sent it to the police, just in case something happens to this one. And I mailed a copy to my lawyer in case he's able to use any of it against Coach Nelson and Will Blake for the shooting."

"Neither the coach nor Will have told the police anything about who killed Scott yet?" Jennifer asked.

"Not a word. Nelson is out on bail, but Will's still locked up. My lawyer convinced the judge to deny bail. Seems odd that one got out and the other didn't, but apparently Nelson has a solid alibi for the night Scott was killed. I think I must have made a huge mistake and prayed for patience. Now I'm being tested."

Kate hugged Cassie. "I think God's working overtime trying to figure this mess out just like the police. Keep your chin up, Cass. At least you and Jameson have happier days ahead to look forward to."

The girls focused on the notebook, reviewing what little they knew about the contents with Detective Rivers when she arrived. Dee filled Nikki in on Cornell's nasty visit to her office and mentioned her recollection about his affair with at least one student.

Nikki's eyebrows raised several times as she read through the notebook, but she was tight-lipped about all other details of the investigation. "We'll add this to the puzzle and see if any of it fits. I know this is getting to be very tedious and alarming to all of you, but it's going very well, considering it's a ten-year-old homicide. Keep in mind, the point-shaving has been going on almost that long, too. Cassie, it looks like you're recovering pretty well. I'm glad to see that. And hopefully, we can get the judge to give us some warrants right away. If we want to look into all of a student's records, where would we go?"

Steff answered. "The registrar's office has most of that, unless it's related to their sports activities. That would be in the athletic department." She shot a glance at Dee, who shrugged.

"Dee," Detective Rivers said as she headed for the

door, "I think it would be wise for you and Lauren to find someplace to stay until all of this is a little more under control. And be sure to avoid a set schedule. Don't come and go at the same time each day. Stay aware of everything that's happening around you.

"We're waiting to see if the crime-scene investigators can get a match on the glove found near your home. They found skin cells inside it, and some skin on the branch. We don't have the authority to order you to do it, but the next step would be to put you under protective custody, for your own safety. Whether you realize it or not, it appears someone thinks you know something."

EIGHTEEN

In her parents' Charleston home, she tried to decide what to do to show him that she meant business. She'd visited her mom and dad in the nursing home this morning so they wouldn't be concerned about her extended absences. Finally she had the place to herself.

He'd promised to send the package two days ago. She had checked the post office box three times. Nothing.

Now he wasn't answering his cell phone. She'd even tried to reach him at the college, but his voice mail there was full, too.

What did that mean?

She looked around the Internet café and took a sip of her coffee. She logged into her French Web mail account and tried again to send the blog entry. *What's wrong? I don't want to log in!* She logged out of the Magnolia College site and then back onto the Where Are They Now Web site directly. She studied it, trying to make sure it was running the same as before.

What a joke. *You girls are lousy Webmasters, by the way.* Nothing looked different.

"That's better," she said. She looked at her daughter's picture and tried to think like Josie.

She went to the blog again and typed in her message.

Hello, Friends. It's so good to hear from all of you, about what's happening in your lives. I'm here in beautiful, romantic Paris, working.

Oh good grief, Josie, what was it you always wanted to do? Something disgustingly simple. What was it?

As an English teacher, like my personal tutor and mentor, Dr. Rutherford.

She laughed to herself, "Nothing like killing two birds with one stone."

It's not quite as romantic as that ski trip we took to Vermont, but it is a good life for me and my adorable daughter. She looks just like her daddy. All my best, friends, and happy memories, Josie S.

NINETEEN

"We've traced the identity of the e-mail account to a Josie Skerritt," Detective Anderson told Edgar and Dee. "Only problem is, the account was set up in France, but we had French authorities run the name and there's no record of any Josie Skerritt ever having lived in France."

Before he asked, Edgar was in the school database to see if Josie had updated her record since graduation. "We don't show any change in the past ten years. You'd need to officially get her information from the registrar's office, but it looks like she may have updated her record a couple of months after graduation."

"Detective Rivers is getting a warrant as we speak. I thought I'd see if either of you can tell me anything about Ms. Skerritt."

"She lived on my floor in the dorm," Dee said. "She was very sweet, fairly quiet—"

Detective Anderson interrupted her. "Can you give

me any details about her? Size? Height? Race? Anything that might help us compare it to the skeleton."

"Oh. Well, she was Caucasian, a little taller than me. I'm five feet six inches. She was thinner than I was, so maybe one hundred thirty pounds. I'm not really sure of that. There were pictures of her in the yearbooks and school newspaper."

The detective nodded. "Thanks, we'll take a look. Close enough for now. Hair, eyes? Anything stand out in her features? Our investigators tried to send the skull off to a forensic artist for reconstruction but until recently, we figured it would go unidentified forever, and that kind of research comes with a hefty price tag."

"What took so long to consider that?" Edgar asked.

"We're a small agency. We couldn't justify spending that kind of money. Since the case has taken so many bizarre turns, we hoped the Georgia Bureau of Investigations would consider footing the bill on it, but they denied our request. Not enough hard evidence. So we're back to what we had before. Who were Josie's closest friends?"

"So why do you think it's Josie?"

"As much as I'd like to say we have a ton of evidence, right now, I can't even say that. It's mostly where these e-mails have sent us next, and a hunch that we're getting to the bottom of a very long list. Good old-fashioned process of elimination. Thankfully, the campus police department has been very cooperative in getting us access to a lot of information we need. That has cut some of the red tape."

Dee couldn't believe the turn this had taken. She tried to focus again, to think about their lives ten years ago. She tried to recall the photographs from the yearbooks at the library. "Ah, Payton Bell, Paige Tatum and Josie were tight friends for a while, Penny Brighton and Josie were close at graduation…" She stopped and her heart skipped a beat. "That's weird, they're all *P.B.* initials."

"Paige Tatum isn't," Edgar said, not even hiding his puzzlement.

"I don't remember when, but she married Will Blake around then. They eventually divorced, but he might know something." Dee looked hopeful, but the detective didn't.

"Will isn't exactly in a talking mood right now, only to say that his ex has their kids and collects far too much alimony."

"I wonder why he hasn't said something about her on the Web site? I'm pretty sure they're among our missing classmates." She opened up the Web site and looked at their list. "Well, everyone except Paige. I guess someone finally posted that she's around."

Edgar was busy looking up each person they mentioned in the school system. He shook his head with each one, sadness darkening his eyes. "No updates to their addresses."

Detective Anderson frowned. "Give us names and we'll get warrants for the rest. So did Josie date much?"

Dee closed her eyes and concentrated on their senior year. Seemed to her that most of them dated quite a few of their classmates, but only a few were serious relationships that went anywhere. "I'm really not sure who, or if anyone was serious. We weren't that close."

"Edgar, you know anything about Josie or Penny?"

"Not really. I recognize a few names from the Campus Christian Fellowship. I was older than most of the people in my class, so I didn't hang out much except for CCF functions."

"And she wasn't part of that group?" Detective Anderson asked.

"Not that I remember," Edgar said.

"Did Josie date anyone casually, then? I mean, whoever this skeleton was, she'd been seeing someone, or she wouldn't have had a baby soon before dying."

"Josie wasn't in my program, so I didn't see her much. I didn't spend much time in the dorms except to sleep."

Jim laughed, and Edgar raised his eyebrow.

"What?" Dee said defensively, looking at Edgar. "You didn't even live on campus."

"I couldn't afford it, and I wasn't required to, since I had a host family."

Detective Anderson cleared his throat. "Did you know of anyone who might have been pregnant at graduation?"

"The only one I'd heard rumors about was Penny Brighton. She and Adam Kessler got married very quickly, which got people talking. Girls like Penny from wealthy families didn't dare show up unwed and pregnant. Then Adam died just a few weeks later in that accident at the lake after graduation. I never heard from Penny again."

"And what about Penny?" Detective Anderson went through the same questions about her vital statistics.

"She was shorter than me, very thin. And moody. One day she would be ecstatic, the next, bawling and yelling at everyone for leaving our laundry in the dryer too long, whatever she could find to complain about. I never could imagine how she and Josie became friends. Or, for that matter, what Cornell Rutherford saw in her."

"Rutherford?" Detective Anderson stared at her. "Are you sure, or is this just gossip?"

Dee nodded. "She made sure we all knew about the affair. One night, she'd been out drinking, and insisted she'd convinced him to leave his wife and family for her. Then all of a sudden, she was with Adam. A few weeks later, they got married. Adam was Steff Kessler's brother. At the time, we were just happy that Penny moved out of the dorm. We were more than a little tired of her drama."

The detective flipped through his notes and shook his head. "Even taking decomposition into consideration, it seems like the height is just a little too short. So what else can you remember about Penny?"

"She was pretty, but was looking for a rich man to take care of her. She was very spoiled and eccentric."

"Hopefully we can track down the girls' families

and see if they can tell us anything. I'm just curious why you didn't mention any of this earlier?"

Dee shrugged. "I didn't even think of it until Professor Rutherford started acting paranoid the other day, to be honest. And well, with the accusations flying on the Web site, memories started coming back. I think I mentioned it to Nikki, but so much has happened, I'm not surprised that it got lost in the hoards of information. I have to admit, I've convinced myself that Rutherford and Penny are involved in this mess somehow. And I'm praying you figure it out soon."

The middle-aged detective nodded. "I appreciate your time. You've been a lot of help. And Miss Owens, be careful. I know Detective Rivers talked to you about finding another place to live temporarily. If you want my opinion, I think that's more of a must than a recommendation. We don't want another case to solve." Detective Anderson left the office, pulling his cell phone from his pocket.

"So," Edgar said with a skeptical grin, "were you as wild as your sister said you were at the time?"

"Nowhere near as crazy as she portrays me," Dee said, crossing her arms over her chest. "But compared to my quiet, conservative sister, I had my share of fun. Being around people has always been the high point of life for me." As Edgar turned toward the door of his office, Dee caught his hand. "But I was at Magnolia College for school. There was no way I was going to let partying, or men, set me back. I had a social life, yes. And I admit that I let Lauren think I was wilder than I really was so she'd leave me alone about going to CCF with her. That was a long time ago and a lot of things have changed now."

"Yes, I'm sure it has. A crisis makes a lot of people turn to God. I know it seems like I'm walking out at a bad time, but I'm running late for an appointment with the provost." The disappointment was evident on Edgar's face as he turned and walked out of the office.

"Anything I should know about?" Dee said as she followed him.

He shrugged. "I'll let you know."

Dee disappeared into her office determined to forget the look of disappointment on Edgar's face. It was harder to ignore his remark about people turning to God in a crisis. Something had obviously given him second thoughts about her.

After trying to focus on work, she finally gave up and went online to read through the new posts from classmates. Everyone was getting more and more curious about the missing co-eds. Most of the messages were requests for information on individuals. The good thing was, the police were now monitoring every word.

Kate Brooks tried a few times to correspond with "Daisy," who kept throwing out snarky accusations about just about everyone in the class. Pretty soon, Jennifer Pappas blocked the posts and told Daisy to stop making trouble. She had posted several more times, eventually dropping accusations that Adam Kessler's boating accident was possibly not an accident. Dee wondered if Steff would respond, or if

Dee should give her a heads-up, since the detective would likely head to her office after the warrants were issued.

This is getting very ugly. Who is so angry?

Dee picked up the phone and dialed Steff. She wasn't there, so Dee left her a message and hoped she reached her in time. A courier from the mailroom knocked on her door and delivered several packages to her in-box.

"Thanks," she said as the kid rushed out of the office, looking in his bag for the next package. "Break is over," she mumbled. "Guess it's time to get back to work."

And though she tried to return to college business, she couldn't stop seeing the disappointment on Edgar's face. She never should have let herself fall for him. Something in Edgar's look this afternoon alarmed her. She thought about his meeting with the provost, wondering how it was going and hoping it had nothing to do with the investigation.

It wasn't long before Dee saw the police return with the warrant for information on more students, she guessed. She stepped out into the hallway. "Detective Anderson, could you come in here when you're done there? I have something else to show you."

She picked up her mail and brought it to the desk to open. The first two packages were campus business, but the third was a box of ashes. With it, someone had cut out words and letters from magazines and newspapers. She read the news clipping of the Burt's Pizza fire from the paper. Then came the personal warning. "Stop the investigation, or the next time it will hit closer to home." At the bottom was a picture of her and Edgar that Sunday morning outside her house.

Detectives Anderson and Rivers came in, and Dee's face paled.

"What's wrong?" Detective Rivers's concern showed on her face and Dee realized she must look like a ghost.

"This just arrived," Dee said as she handed Nikki the note.

The two of them read the note and shook their heads. "Dee, I'm sorry. Do you know when this picture was taken?"

"Right before we came to the station Sunday morning. Steff and Lauren were inside, and I ran out for just a second," she said, every emotion of that minute coming back in full color. In the photo, Edgar was holding her hand, and she was wearing her robe. But it looked like he was leaving and she was crying over him going. Dee dropped her face into her hands. "That isn't what it looks like, really."

"Have you shown it to anyone else?"

Dee shook her head. "It had to have been what Cornell Rutherford was talking about. He had to have sent this."

"We'll look into it right away. It arrived with this box, in this envelope?"

She nodded.

"Could I have one of those new envelopes to put it all into?"

Dee pulled one out and Nikki Rivers moved the evidence into a new manilla envelope.

Dee took a deep breath as the letter and box disappeared from view. "What I called you back for, though, was to look at the most recent blog posts." While she talked, the two detectives began reading the entries. "This is getting out of control. Steff Kessler might have an idea who, besides Penny Brighton, would have this kind of information about her brother's death. Also, I think the time has come to disable the blog. It's becoming nothing more than a free-for-all."

Detective Rivers shook her head. "I'll see if the techs have blocked anything, then see if we can do something to make it private, at least. I just hate to turn off our main source of information."

Edgar walked into the room, a scowl on his face. "This has got to end."

"You saw today's posts, I presume," Dee said, looking up at Detective Anderson. "I just asked if we could temporarily take it offline. Hopefully the police have enough leads now to find this person and make an arrest."

"I hope so, because this person is scandalizing everyone in our class." He looked at Dee, then the detective. "This wasn't how we thought the Web site would turn out, Detective, and it's going to kill the college."

Dee sent Nikki Rivers a silent plea. "Edgar needs to see the latest."

"As soon as we finish the discussion on the blog.

We're this close to finding 'Daisy,'" Nikki said, holding her finger and thumb barely apart. "We've sent an officer to apprehend the computer where the posts have been sent from. Give us a few more days. Dee, I'm fine with you trying to calm this person down, or even if you post a disclaimer, we'll insert that every few posts, so readers will realize this is not reflective of the quality of students, whatever you want to say, that's fine, but we need her to keep spouting off. She knows what happened, and we have to locate her through the Web site. It really is our best avenue."

"Edgar?" Dee said. She clung to the hope that he would agree. If they wanted to catch whoever was doing this, they had to let the police run this their way.

"What's the latest?"

Dee felt her stomach turn. "A box of ashes and a note."

"And what did it say?"

The detective put on a glove and pulled it out far enough for Edgar to read it and see the photo.

"Four days," he said, his voice firm as he turned and left Dee's office.

The detectives watched Edgar storm out of the office. Nikki Rivers turned to Dee. "Miss Owens, I'm not going to mince words. You need to find someplace to live here in the middle of town. We can't guarantee your safety anywhere, but especially not twenty minutes outside town."

Dee felt her heart beat out of control. "You really think that's necessary?"

"Only if you value your life," Detective Rivers said firmly. "And that of your loved ones. When you make a decision, let me know. We'll want to orchestrate it so it isn't obvious."

Loved ones—her family, friends, Edgar. How could she protect Edgar now? If it wasn't for her running outside in her robe, Cornell would have had nothing to hold over their heads. She had to talk to Edgar and apologize.

"Dee, are you listening? We should make this move as soon as possible. I'm going to have a cruiser go by the house and make sure it's okay."

"I should be able to load up my car inside the garage."

Nikki nodded. "Good. I also want to install a few cameras around the property."

Dee nodded. "I'll call Lauren, see how soon she can meet me. I'll call you and let you know when we'll be going out there."

"Good, I'll get the supplies ready and ride out with you. That way no one will see anything out of the ordinary."

She was frightened before. Now she was terrified.

TWENTY

Per the detective's request, Dee had said nothing to anyone about the package. Not even to her sister. She'd told Lauren simply that she'd thought about what Lauren and Seth had said, and felt they were right. It wasn't an hour before Dee and Lauren had packed a few bags and moved into the spare bedroom at Seth's house, as Nikki Rivers had suggested. Nowhere would she be able to take Tipsy. Even here, Dee would have to make the cat live in the garage to avoid triggering Seth's son's allergies, so she left Tipsy at home with extra food and water. She would stop by in a few days to make sure the cat was doing okay.

Edgar wouldn't return her calls and, according to his office, was out of town for a few days.

The police had installed automatic timers so the lights would turn on and off on a regular basis and set up their own security cameras at her house just in case something happened. Whoever was trying to scare her didn't stand a chance of getting away without being caught now.

So far, thanks to the help of technology and co-workers, she'd worked from her future brother-in-law's house for three days, staying totally out of sight.

This was, to her, as difficult as speaking in front of a crowd was for her sister. Every time Lauren and Seth both left the house, Dee turned the television or radio up a notch louder. Being alone and out of the limelight had never been such torture.

The letters Dee and Steff had been working on were finally ready, thanks to Edgar's lighting a fire under the IT department to tweak the coding errors in the database. Lauren had picked them up when she'd gone shopping for groceries.

Lauren was busy in the kitchen as soon as she finished unloading the car. While she worked in the kitchen, Dee worked at the dining room table.

"How about going to church with us tonight for the prayer vigil?"

Dee had been expecting this. Even though she'd made her personal peace with God, she wasn't in any mood right now for a public display, especially not after Edgar's snide remark about people turning to God during a crisis. What if he was right? What if she was just as guilty of using God as a crutch as the people she'd been so upset with?

"Not tonight, thanks anyway."

"If you're worried about the stalker, I highly doubt the person would follow you to church."

"You don't watch the news much, do you? Crimes

happen in churches as much as they do anywhere else."

Lauren put her hands on her hips. "So does that mean you won't go anywhere there's crime?"

"I didn't say that at all. I said not tonight."

"Why not?"

Dee knew of no other way to say it. "The Rutherfords go there. I don't think I can face him, Lauren. It's beyond me how he could even show his face in a church." Dee eyed the pastries that Lauren had just taken from the oven. She examined each one, as if judging them for a contest.

"The church doesn't close its doors to anyone, so we shouldn't, either. We're all sinners in some way. Besides, I haven't seen Dr. Rutherford in church since I've been here. He drops his son off and leaves."

"Aha!" Dee said with a burst of energy, making her sister jump. "So I might have to see him," she said, and she ate a bite of her sister's pastries. "These are good, but they're a little sweet."

"That's why they're for dessert. You've got to stop eating or you're going to lose that to-die-for figure, Dee. And then you won't fit into your maid-of-honor dress."

"You haven't even set a date," she complained. "I thought if I moved in, you were going to move the date up."

Lauren shrugged. "I thought we would, but I don't want this cloud hanging over us on such a wonderful day. It's been more than ten years, what's a few more weeks? Besides, I have so many other things to focus on right now, it's keeping my mind off it."

"You can cross me off your list, Lauren. I appreciate Seth letting us stay here for a few days, but I can take care of myself. It was Nikki Rivers's idea for me to get out of the house. Not mine."

"You surely aren't going to argue with that, are you?" Lauren leaned across the counter and stared at her sister. "I know it is difficult for you to let someone else take care of you," she said. "Look at the bright side—we could have Mom and Dad staying with us."

Dee could always count on her sister to find a way to cheer her up. "That's true. The last thing I need is to worry about someone else becoming a target. Somehow, we've got to help the police catch whoever is doing this." She went to the refrigerator and got a glass of milk.

"I think we need to let them handle it. We need to pray that God will empower Nikki and Jim to solve these cases. What really concerns me is we don't even know why this stalker is after us."

Dee shook her head, determined to keep the warning to herself. She was just happy it hadn't shown up on the blog or on some news station. For now, she had to try to put it out of her mind. That was next to impossible.

"Depending on who I suspect, I have a few ideas. Number one is someone who thinks we know too much. I just wish we knew what we know." As she realized how that came out, she got a puzzled look on her face and laughed.

"Okay, you're getting some definite cabin fever when you start talking nonsense like that. Dee, just think about going tonight, would you, please?"

"I appreciate the offer, but I have so many other things on my mind right now. The insurance company still hasn't approved a rental car." Not to mention, recruiting, the Web site and Edgar, she thought. He'd put a time limit of four days on keeping the blog live, and they were on day three.

"How soon till your car is repaired?" Lauren put the next pan of pastries into the oven and started cleaning up the dishes, making enough racket to wake the dead.

Dee tore her mind from Edgar. "They estimated two weeks, give or take a few days. I think I may as well get a rental. I can't sit around here for that long letting you and Seth chauffeur me." Dee pulled out a tea towel and dried the oversize pans.

"It's not that big of a problem. I feel much better knowing you're with someone most of the time. I remember how it was when Reese was following me. It's the least I can do to repay your hospitality and support." When they were done with the dishes, Lauren followed Dee to the dining room table and they returned to the letter-stuffing project.

"I heard from Steff that the police have been all over campus the last couple of days. They questioned a few more faculty members. They even questioned an administrative assistant with the initials of P.B., so they're being very thorough. I just hope it's not a long list of suspects. I wonder if they've found anything about Payton Bell yet," Dee said absently, willing to say anything to try to get her mind off Edgar.

"According to Cassie, they had a warrant to look into the records of the players in her brother's notebook. They've started questioning them, too. Sounds like it's sure to come to a head soon."

"I hope so. This is getting so frustrating. I need to get back to my life, not sit here stuffing envelopes while I'm in hiding."

"While you're working there, think about going with us to the prayer vigil tonight. God is always with you, Dee, even when you think you've put up a wall around yourself. You've always been His. When you think you've been off creating your career, He's always been there. It's kind of like those computer programs, working and keeping things running in the background."

"I'm finding that out. The walls are just crumbling around me, in a good way, and I'm a little surprised to see how much differently I see things as an adult."

Lauren looked puzzled.

"Remember Annie?"

Lauren nodded. "Your friend who had cancer, right?"

"Yeah." Dee explained how she'd seen and perceived Annie's parents' messages at the time. "I could see her family walking the walk, saying everything right, and I was just sure that it was me who wasn't praying right, because if they thought God couldn't use a doctor's hands to heal Annie, how could our prayers heal her. I realize now, I probably don't know everything that they tried. I just saw that they claimed God would heal her and it looked like they didn't let the doctors try radiation or chemo. I was so angry…" Her tears flowed. "I promised I'd never use God as a crutch. I did everything I could, whether it be for my health, or for my friends, or my career. And in the midst of doing everything I could, I closed out God. Now, I'm afraid I'm the one using Him as a crutch."

Lauren paused what she was working on and came and sat down with Dee. "It's a fine line, isn't it? I mean, we're told to turn our lives over to Him, to rely fully on Him, yet when does that become a 'crutch'? Or does it?" She thought longer. "That's a tough question."

"For a while it was out-and-out rebellion, and then it was just too hard to go back and realize how wrong I was to close Him out when I needed Him the most. And now, how do I make time? I don't exactly have a nine-to-five job, can get called out at just about any time of day or night…" She started to go on, but Lauren cleared her throat.

"When something is important, you make time. I know that, since I've been back with Seth, I don't spend nearly as much time as I used to worrying about things."

"I wasn't talking about romance," Dee said.

"I didn't mean just romance, Dee. Seth and I share our commitment to make God the center of our lives, so that helps take away the stress of worrying about making time for two things, because we can be together and study the Bible, or go to church and be together."

"How nice," Dee said, feeling totally overwhelmed by the thought of making any changes in her life. "And how over my head right now, sorry. I'm way back in Christianity 101, I think."

"It's just like anything else, one step at a time. For now, ask God into your heart to stay. You make that commitment, and everything else will fall into place."

"I know. Maybe it's just all of this other stuff happening right now that has me feeling so doubtful. It has always bothered me when people just sit back and expect God to fix everything without applying themselves. And now, I think that's what I'm doing. I'm afraid, and…" She finished putting labels on the last envelope. "My, I wish they could have personalized these letters so we could have used window envelopes instead."

Lauren finished cleaning up her baking mess and started to help stuff the envelopes. "I hear what you're saying. You always made it look so easy, studying and a busy social life, beauty and brains. There's no way you could ever sit back and expect something to be handed to you on a golden platter. God knows that, Dee. He knows what's in your heart. He knows that you've had a full plate lately, and yet here you are putting stamps and labels on envelopes at home. You're not hiding out from the enemy and feeling sorry for yourself. You're giving it your all."

"But I can't go to the prayer service with you. And I hate feeling like I'm wanting a handout."

"Do you believe that God loves you?"

Dee nodded.

"Do you love Him and trust Him?"

Dee looked at her. "Lauren, I never stopped. Not in my heart anyway. I'd pull out my Bible and read it now and then. I'd question God, and I wasn't nearly as wild in college as you thought I was. I didn't want to go to CCF with you, and listen to people sit there Sunday night and pray for a good grade instead of going home and studying to earn it. To me, that wasn't using the gifts God gave us." She finished her spiel and let out a gust of air. "I'm sorry I let you worry about me all these years. And now, even though I want to change, I'm terrified to do it."

"Maybe it would make you even stronger if you could bring your relationship with God to the front of your life now. You have a successful career, and you've got your home to where you like it. Once this is over, you can probably pick up where you'd like to with Edgar. You might be surprised that you have even more time than you did before."

Dee pushed her hair behind her ear and wiped tears from her face. "I think Edgar's realized we're not right for each other. And even if he changes his mind, I don't know if I can deal with a romantic relationship and getting right with God at the same time. Maybe God just doesn't mean for me to be married. I mean, a lot of people are happily single."

"Well, yes, that may be a possibility. So it isn't just that Cornell Rutherford might be there tonight—it's Edgar, too?"

She shrugged. "I believe he's still out of town, but that will definitely be a factor in me going to Magnolia Church in the future." Dee just couldn't think any more about Edgar right now. She'd thought for sure they were going somewhere, until they'd been unable to take the blog off of the Web site. Until that photo appeared.

Dee leaned over to Lauren and wrapped her arms around her. "Thank you for being here, for letting me show my weaknesses to you."

"It's not a weakness to let me take care of you for a change, Dee. That's healthy, for both of us. And it's natural for you to be overthinking your faith in the middle of this. Sometimes God allows us to be weak so that we realize we need to turn our troubles over to Him. I can't help but think you'd be that person on the roof of the house who arrives in Heaven and asks God why He didn't save you."

"That's not funny."

"No, it's not, but it was funny when God said 'I sent two boats and a helicopter, what more did you want?' You're so used to being in control, and sometimes you have to let someone else take charge, and you be the follower. Sometimes God sends someone else in to help us, and we need to let them."

"It might be a little of that, too." She thought of Edgar, of the fact that he realized already that she wanted to be the one holding the information. Still, his last accusation stung.

It was hardly fair of him to make a personal judgment on her based upon a two-minute conversation.

They'd been at work, hardly the appropriate place to discuss her social life in college or her faith. He'd barely been in touch with her since, and then, only to discuss work issues. So if that was what was keeping him from talking to her on a personal level, it was best she know now.

She knew a lot of relationships broke apart because of differences in faith. Edgar probably felt she'd strayed too far to come back. Maybe she had, but she didn't think so, and it made it that much more difficult to think he'd come to such a conclusion. After all, she'd have gone into far more detail if she and a man were discussing a future together in a private conversation. Of course she'd want a future husband to know why she'd strayed from God, why she'd wanted nothing to do with CCF in those days. She wanted to tell him, but he didn't seem to want to listen.

She was fuming all over again. He hadn't even let her explain, had simply jumped to the conclusion that her faith wouldn't last.

There was only one way to know for sure, and that wouldn't be apparent until long after these threats were gone. Until she could convince him that her reunion with God was more than her desperately reaching out for a crutch during a crisis, how could she let herself fall deeper in love with him?

"Dee, you can't let other people dictate your relationship with God—for the positive or negative. Like anywhere on earth, the church is filled with humans who have individual needs and battles to fight. I think that is our strength as a community. We can draw on one anothers' strengths and pray for each other's struggles..."

Dee's mind strayed again to her feelings for Edgar. Why hadn't she called him, made him listen?

"...if Cornell is involved in these crimes, I highly doubt he'd come tonight to pray that he, himself, get put to justice."

Dee laughed nervously. Her mind was so far from Cornell right now she didn't dare admit to her sister that she hadn't heard half of what she'd been saying. "That would be worth seeing. I'll consider it, Lauren. It's about time I clear my mind and ask God to help me walk with Him through good times and bad."

"Good," Lauren replied, seeming somewhat surprised. "If you need anything let me know. I'll be in the bedroom, cleaning." Lauren disappeared down the hall.

Dee buckled down to finish her project, hoping they could put them in the mail drop when they went to pick Jake up from school. She read her e-mail, focusing on the one from Edgar giving his plans for the recruiting fair in Charleston. She was somewhat hesitant about going now, after receiving that photo, but she also needed to get away from Magnolia Falls. She was able to rearrange her other appointments to fit Edgar's recruiting schedule for the three days, and she hoped it would give them a chance to talk.

Since time was running so short, she called Parker Buchanan and proposed the idea of joining them in Charleston. She gave him the date and held her breath. "Please, Parker. It would be a great chance to promote your next comic book."

"You don't have to spin it to me, Dee. I think I have some time. Plus it would be good to get away from here for a couple of days. This investigation is getting too strange. It's hard to imagine Magnolia Falls without the college."

"Yes it is, isn't it?"

Parker responded hesitantly, "You don't think it would get that bad, do you?"

"In this economy, stranger things have happened, but we're not going to let it go without a fight." Dee was giddy with excitement about convincing the millionaire recluse, Parker Buchanan, to speak about the college.

"These scandals certainly have brought the fight out in everyone. And it sure looks as if someone has it in for Dr. Rutherford. Any idea who that is?"

Parker Buchanan—P.B. Dee was very careful to remain calm. "No, I don't have a clue. Parker, thank you again, so much. I'll have Edgar Ortiz, the interim director of admissions, give you a call with the travel plans."

"Sounds good. I'll see you next week."

Dee turned on the television and caught a special report interrupting a game show with breaking news. "…a professor and dean at Magnolia College in Magnolia Falls have been arrested by the Magnolia Falls Police Department on several charges related to the death of Scott Winters, journalist for the

Savannah Herald. We'll have more details on the five-o'clock news."

Dee felt light-headed and gasped for air. Her cell phone rang immediately. She didn't recognize the number, but it looked like one from the college. "Hello."

"Dee, this is J. T. Kessler. Looks like we have more damage to spin."

"I just heard the news report, or part of it. Who was arrested?"

"Rutherford. That's only half of it. Get here as soon as you can."

"Did Cornell kill the girl, too?"

"They haven't said that yet. We'll fill you in when you get here. How soon will that be?"

"Ten or fifteen minutes." She gathered her purse as she headed toward the door, then realized she didn't have a car and she wasn't dressed to go on television. "Ah, make that half an hour." Dee closed her phone and glanced in the mirror at the entrance. "Lauren, I need to go to the college, right away!" She rushed into the bedroom and found her sister. "They've arrested Rutherford."

Lauren's jaw fell open. "What?"

Dee repeated the information as she changed into a suit and touched up her makeup.

"You were right!"

"We don't know for sure that he did any of it yet, just that he's a suspect, although they did make an arrest," Dee said as she reached for the door handle. "Let's hope this is the beginning of the end."

* * *

Edgar left the recruiting fair at four o'clock, exhausted. It had been a long and lonely day. He had hoped he'd be able to rehire some of the recruiters that they'd had to let go this week, but if things didn't turn around soon, that wasn't going to be a possibility. He'd realized their numbers would be down, but he didn't think it would hit this hard, this soon. He was beginning to wonder if it would be a blessing in disguise if he didn't get the director's position.

The provost was concerned about not only Edgar's chances, but the hope of saving the school overall. The board of trustees had decided they weren't even going to bring in candidates for interviews until the new fiscal year, when they had a better idea of their chances to recover. That meant Edgar would remain as interim director for five more months. The good side of that was he had time to bring the school out of this hole. They had time to evaluate the damage. And he had time to figure out if he and Dee stood a chance together.

He walked into the lobby of the hotel, greeted by Dee's ashen face on the television. "What's happened?" Edgar asked the clerk who was glued to the television.

"They arrested someone for conspiracy or something," she answered.

Edgar moved across the room and listened carefully. Though she looked tired, he could see some relief on her face. There was a light in her eyes that had been absent the past few weeks. He wasn't sure if he was happier to see her safe or that they were right about the Cornell case breaking soon.

"Magnolia Falls Police Department have placed Cornell Rutherford, dean of the liberal arts college, under arrest today for alleged charges in relation to the point-shaving scheme, conspiracy in the murder of Scott Winters, and conspiracy to commit murder in the shootings of Scott's sister, Cassie Winters, Professor Jameson King and former Magnolia College basketball player, Kevin Reed."

Poor David. This will crush him.

Dee was holding up extremely well, especially considering her personal involvement in the case. He never should have done this to her.

"Following due process, as stated in the policies of the college, Dean Rutherford has been placed on immediate leave from his duties. The board of trustees will appoint an interim dean within the week.

"The Magnolia Falls Police Department is also questioning several persons of interest in the investigation of the skeleton found months ago, thanks to the lead found on the charm. Investigators expect to have an identity of the victim very soon.

"The faculty and staff would again like to thank the community of Magnolia Falls for their assistance, patience and prayers throughout these investigations. We would also like to commend the Magnolia Falls Police Department for their service securing the campus of Magnolia College and making it one of the safest colleges in Georgia." The reporter cut Dee off.

No questions were allowed, apparently. Just like

that, Dee was gone and they'd moved on to another breaking story.

What did she know that they hadn't let her say in the announcement? Had they also charged Rutherford with stalking? With the murder? As soon as he reached his room, Edgar tried to contact Dee. Apparently, so was everyone else, as her voice mail box was full. He couldn't even let her know he'd heard the news.

While he was relieved that they'd made progress on the cases, he couldn't help wondering when all this would end. When would they begin to see the light again?

Edgar closed his work folder and pulled his Bible from his suitcase. He began to look for some way to encourage David Rutherford through this difficult time. He wanted more than anything to go home right away and see Dee and Christiana, make sure they were really okay, but he knew the board of trustees wouldn't look favorably on him backing away from recruiting. Especially not now.

He reached his sister and talked to her at length about how David was handling his father's arrest. It didn't sound good. His mother, Madelain Kessler, had picked him up at school right before the news was made public, and Christiana hadn't been able to reach him since.

Edgar hated having to have this emotional conversation with her long distance, but he was thankful that Christiana was staying with Pastor Rogers and his family for the week. At least he knew she would have a good listener available when he wasn't around. "Christiana, send David an e-mail and let him know he can call me at any time if he needs someone to listen. I'm sure his mother is trying to protect the kids right now. He probably has no clue that you've tried to call him."

"Can I text him?" she said, fear in her voice. "Just this once, Edgar. Please. He needs to know I'm here for him."

So far, he hadn't encountered the same problems with his sister's cell phone as most teenager's parents did. She respected the limits they lived with. She'd grown up without many of the privileges that her friends had. He suspected that made all the difference. Would allowing it this time open up problems? "What's wrong with an e-mail?"

"The police took all of their computers."

"Oh." Edgar hadn't thought about that. "Texting adds up very fast, Christiana. Only one text to tell him to call you when he wants to. That's really about all you can do at this point. It may take him some time to feel like talking to anyone."

An hour later, Dee called to share the news personally, and it was a comfort to hear her voice. Even though he was relieved that they had one more piece of the puzzle, he still wondered where they would land on a personal note after all the fallout.

"You sound tired," she said. "Are you okay, Edgar?"

"Enrollment is going to be even worse than we expected," he admitted finally.

"This arrest gives us a lot of room for improvement though. It shows progress, and we can revisit our strategy when you get back."

He couldn't seem to comprehend how Cornell Rutherford could be behind this. "It shows corruption right up to the top. Can't you do something more to spin this?"

"Like what, Edgar? Do you want me to beat around the bush, spread some rumors and prove the naysayers true, that we're trying to sweep the truth under the rug?" Her disgust was very clear.

"Of course not, but there has to be some way to avoid saying the same thing that the police are reporting. That just reinforces the negative."

There was a long silence on the other end of the phone. "Is that really what you expect of me, Edgar? To squirm like a snake and charm the public into believing we were covering up these crimes? I know I have a nickname as the Queen of Spin, Edgar, but I told you up front when we discussed the best strategy that I'm not a spin doctor. I'm one of the best because I sandwich the good with the bad, say something good before, sandwich in the bad, and end on a positive note. Maybe you've got the wrong person after all."

"Dee, I'm sorry. I wasn't thinking. No, of course that isn't the way I meant to say it." He couldn't believe he'd asked her to avoid the truth. "It's been a very long, discouraging day. The looks in students' eyes seems almost accusing. Now I find out it really is the man you suspected, and I didn't want to believe it was possible."

"No," she said, "I never suspected he was involved with the point-shaving, but there's only one way to dispel questions, Edgar. With the truth. Magnolia College is the best small college in Georgia, in all the South, even. We'll win a lot more loyalty back with honesty than bad PR tactics. The students were celebrating today. They feel better just knowing Rutherford is going to face justice, that he can't keep blackmailing his students."

"They have a false sense of security, then, because I don't believe that Rutherford is a murderer. Someone may still be out there. Shouldn't we tell them that rather than let them think Cornell is our fall guy?"

Dee was quiet. "It seems no matter how I do it, you want this job done differently. It's my observation that the community doesn't want to be told how to think. They can reason that we didn't say there's still a murderer out there. They know we've had multiple crimes to investigate. I'm not telling them lies."

"What else did the police say, off the record?"

"They hope to get a DNA sample so they can see if the glove at my house was his, but they aren't sure how long that might take. Reese Morton has been questioned and is a key witness, so they have moved her to a safe location, and the case against him on the point-shaving is pretty solid.

"As for the skeleton," she continued, "the police gave me specifically what I could say, Edgar."

"So we'd better pray that more charges follow soon."

"They expect an identity of the skeleton any time now," she said, defending herself and the police.

"And the blog?"

Dee sounded tired and irritated. "You gave them until tomorrow afternoon. Surely you're not going back on your word?"

"Not at all. I wanted to make sure you take a look at the posting today. It looks like Daisy definitely has an ax to grind with Cornell."

"That's nothing we didn't already know."

The watcher stared at the television, watching Goody Two-shoes announcing Cornell Rutherford's arrest. "Good, at least if I can't make use of you, nobody will, not even your wife!"

She packed a bag and prepared to disappear again. It was going to be tougher this time. *Those nosy classmates are getting too involved. Dee, I don't know where you disappeared to, but I'm not going to stop until the job is finished. Cornell was a weakling, but not me.*

Now it's time to quiet all of you down.

TWENTY-ONE

Nikki Rivers walked into Dee's office the next afternoon with a young woman. "Dee Owens?" she said as Dee looked up to see a young face of Josie Skerritt.

Dee gasped. It was such a shock to see her, here. "Josie, it's so good to see you."

The woman extended her hand. "I'm not Josie. I'm Shelley Skerritt Johnson. Josie's sister."

"This is the woman who called you a few weeks ago."

"Oh," Dee said, breathless to be facing the woman belonging to the voice that had haunted her. "I don't know what to say. Have a seat, please."

"I want to thank you for listening, Dee. I didn't realize what a bad connection we had that night, but according to Detective Rivers, you couldn't hear most of what I said."

"No, but you're here now. Did you find anything out about your sister?"

Shelley looked to Detective Rivers, who answered,

"Yes, we did. Shelley, it's up to you how much you want revealed at this point."

"Detective Rivers first called me in Florida, but it's the kind of call that you really hate to admit how relieved you are to get. At least now, if this is Josie, we know. It wasn't like Josie to hold a grudge. She had to have known Mom and Dad were just reacting to the shock of hearing her news about the baby."

Dee leaned forward. "I don't understand. What baby? When?"

"Josie came home a couple of weeks before graduation and told us that she was pregnant. My parents were disgraced. They didn't want anyone to know. They asked who the father was, and Josie refused to tell any of us. She said it was just one of those things that happened. She and the father weren't really dating, they were both just needing comfort one night, and it ended up going too far. She didn't want to ruin his life."

"So you still don't know who the father is? Do you know what happened to Josie after that?"

Shelley shook her head. "Not really. Mom and Dad refused to help her out, and she ran, promised never to come back. I wanted to help, but our parents threatened to cut me off and not pay for school if I had any contact with her. We were able to e-mail each other, but ten years ago, even that was pretty limited. I got a card from her a few months later. She included this picture of her daughter."

Inside was an infant's photo. A sweet, innocent face that looked a lot like her mother's.

Shelley held it up to Dee, and then to Nikki. "It looks a lot like the photo that is inside the locket," the officer whispered. "That in itself isn't conclusive, since the initials don't match your sister's, but it's a start. With Shelley's help, we've found their family dentist and expect a positive identification from the dental records soon."

Tears welled in Shelley's eyes, matching Dee's. Dee pulled some tissues from the desk drawer and offered some to Shelley. "I'm so sorry, Shelley." Dee offered a hug, a little surprised when Shelley accepted it.

"At least we know."

"Wait until we get the results back," Detective Rivers warned them. "We'll know soon enough."

"In my heart, I knew it was her the minute I heard about the skel—discovery. Now I need to find my niece. I need for her to know that we loved her mother. I want to tell her about Josie. And if we can't find her father, my husband and I want to take her in. My parents are going to have to get over it, to realize that this little girl is all they have left of Josie."

The room turned eerily quiet.

"Dee, thank you for seeing us. I'll let you know as soon as we have a positive ID," Detective Rivers said. "We have an appointment at the library to go through the archives. I'd like to see if any names sound familiar to Shelley."

"Sure, that will be helpful. I went through them a few weeks ago, the night you called me, in fact." She recalled everything from that night. "Here's my business card, if you want to talk or have questions. Are you going to be here for a while? I'd like to get some of Josie's college friends together."

"I'm only staying a couple of days, but that would be nice. I heard so much about all of you from Josie. I wanted to come to Magnolia College, but when Josie got pregnant and disappeared, I couldn't do that to the family. I knew it would be too painful."

The thought of losing Lauren sent chills up Dee's spine. The idea of walking over that sidewalk, realizing Josie had been under there for so many years made her nauseous.

"Let's plan on dinner tonight at seven, um, eight. There's a prayer vigil at Magnolia Christian Church tonight. Maybe you'd like to go to it before dinner?" Dee hoped she could talk Lauren into letting her borrow her car.

"I appreciate the invitation, but if anyone realizes who I am, it may create a media frenzy over nothing. It may not be my sister. And if Mom and Dad saw me on the news, they would freak out. I've had to handle this all very carefully with them. Eight will be fine for dinner."

"Okay, I'm not sure how many of the girls can make it, but if no one else can come, we'll still have dinner together. May I pick you up somewhere?"

"I'd love that. I'm at the B and B on Peach Tree Lane. And Dee, thank you again for passing my concerns on to the police."

"We're going to get to the bottom of this, Shelley. I promise." Dee watched the two leave the office and let the news sink in. *Josie Skerritt. She was so quiet and nice, who'd want to kill her? And who has her baby?*

Dee called to get the girls together for supper, luring them into changing plans by announcing they had a possible identity of the skeleton. Kate was the only one of the six of them who couldn't make it, as she was filling in for another nurse.

She stopped at Edgar's office before leaving the building to fill him in on the latest. "Hi, I thought I saw you walk in."

He barely glanced up. "I'm just here for a few minutes. What can I do for you?"

She had hoped to spend some time with him, but he appeared determined to keep his distance. "I thought I'd fill you in on the latest."

"More pictures?"

"No. Nothing more has surfaced on that, thank God." While it broke her heart that he was shutting her out, she tried not to let her pain show. She wanted him, but not at the expense of his career. "How were your visits today?" she asked.

"Slightly better, but no commitments yet. There was lots of talk about the school making it on the news."

Dee hoped he could somehow bring their enrollment numbers closer to normal. "At this point, I think the news has to get better. It's not official yet, but the police expect dental records to verify that it's Josie Skerritt."

He remained silent for a few minutes. "I had hoped

they were wrong, that it was a much older skeleton than ten years, that maybe it was just..."

"An accident?"

"I was thinking 'well preserved.'" He shook his head and glanced up at Dee. "I didn't know she was pregnant."

Dee shrugged. "Apparently you're not alone. Her family knew about the baby, but her parents shunned her, and they never heard from her again.

"The police finally found her family and now her sister is here, going through details. She brought Josie's dental records with her."

"How is she?"

"She's upset, but also relieved to know why her sister just disappeared. She's the person who called me that night we met at the library."

"Does she have any idea as to who might have killed Josie?" Edgar asked.

"I don't know, we haven't talked that much yet. Nikki Rivers was with her. A bunch of us girls are going to get together at the Terra Cottage for dinner, kind of a chance to piece things together and share some memories about Josie."

"I'd say have a nice time, but it doesn't sound quite right. Be careful, Dee." He turned back to his computer and Dee left.

The women all met at the quiet Italian restaurant near the bed-and-breakfast where Shelley was staying. Dee had been able to reserve a private room, and introduced Josie's sister to everyone as they arrived, watching as they figured out that Josie was the victim.

As soon as they ordered, Shelley explained what she knew about her sister's disappearance. What she wanted to know was about who her sister might have been dating at the time she was killed.

No one remembered for sure, but several names were thrown out.

"Detective Rivers and I went to the library to look at the yearbooks and newspapers, but the years that we needed were gone."

"Gone? They were there a few weeks ago," Dee insisted. "I just looked at them the night you called me. Did you check with the librarian? Maybe they were—"

"That's the weird thing," Shelley said. "They had a break-in a few weeks ago. When the police arrived, they found a pile of ashes but weren't able to determine what had been destroyed. The vandal didn't leave any fingerprints."

Jennifer looked at the others. "That's more than odd. Do you know how close that was to when we had the flames on the blog?"

Dee pulled her calendar from her purse and looked at her records. "It was just a few days after that."

"What's that?" Shelley asked. "Was anyone hurt?"

Cassie explained the situation. "After the skeleton was found, my brother was investigating the story and happened upon evidence of a point-shaving scheme with the college basketball team. He got close enough to scare the suspects, and they killed him.

"I was shot trying to find the person who killed my brother, and Dee and Lauren have been attacked and threatened, too. Among the threats was a blog post of our class-reunion picture with electronic flames flickering in front of all of us."

"Ah, yes. I remember someone discussing that on the blog, but I never actually saw it. This is all getting rather creepy, isn't it?"

"That's putting it mildly." Lauren hadn't said much up till now. "So, Shelley, you said you'd kind of kept in touch with Josie. When was the last time you heard anything from her?"

"Well, right before graduation she came to move some of her things home. That's when we found out she was pregnant. She was sick the whole weekend. Mom and Dad were insistent that they know who the father was or they wouldn't go to graduation. No matter how I tried to sneak away to go, I wasn't able to pull it off. They watched me like a hawk." She shook her head. "I was scheduled to start college here in the fall, but they refused to let me come, and threatened to take away my college fund if I did anything to help Josie. So the only way we could communicate was through e-mail. Even then I didn't dare check my account from home for fear my parents would see. I spent a lot of time at a friend's house that summer, e-mailing her. But in those days we were all on limited time dial-up for Internet, and I couldn't use all of my friend's time. Besides, Josie didn't have a computer, so she was checking hers at Internet cafés or libraries, too."

"Where'd she go after graduation?"

"She and another pregnant friend were going to

Europe, but I don't think they did. Josie didn't have any money, and she was so sick that first trimester that I don't think she would have gotten on an airplane. That's one of the things that doesn't make sense in the e-mails from Josie," Shelley said, using her hands to put quotes around her sister's name. "She was terrified of flying and had no desire to see any of Europe."

"That's right," Jennifer said. "When I was trying to get some teaching students to go with me to Latin America for a summer to teach in an orphanage, she refused."

Lauren frowned. "Did she say who the friend was?"

"I suppose, but I don't remember now, that was so long ago. It was some girl who had just gotten married and was pregnant, but something happened to her husband..."

Steff gasped. "Penny."

"What did you say?"

Shelley looked at her as Steff repeated the name.

"Yes, I think that's who it was. Penny..."

"Penny Brighton...Kessler. P.B.," Dee whispered. "So there's a picture of Josie's baby in Penny's charm? Why wouldn't she have used *P.K.* for Kessler? Or did she get the charm before she and Adam married? Did she take back her maiden name after your brother died, Steff?"

"I haven't a clue. She came to tell us she was expecting Adam's child, but she wasn't showing at all and she was supposedly three to four months along by then. Anyway, Penny claimed she needed financial help to make sure the Kessler child would be raised properly. Mom insisted she was lying, and we never saw Penny again." Steff glanced at Shelley. "Penny always wanted money. We think that's why she married Adam in the first place."

"What happened to your brother?" Shelley asked.

"He was killed in a boating accident at a graduation party."

"Yes, that sounds right," Shelley said. "Penny..."

"Brighton," Dee finished. "It sounds like a fair assumption that she isn't using Kessler around here, anyway."

"I ran into Penny a few years ago, with a little girl," Shelley said. "Penny looked at me like she was seeing a ghost. Like you did this afternoon, Dee."

Dee felt a tap on the shoulder and jumped.

"Dee," Edgar said quietly. "I'm sorry to interrupt, but we need you to make the announcement on the ten-o'clock news." He glanced up and looked right at Shelley. "It is Josie. I'm very sorry."

A hush fell over the table.

"I knew," she said, releasing a breath. "I knew my sister wouldn't have stayed away. Not from me, anyway. Now we can finally have closure and find her little girl. I want to make sure she knows about her mother."

"Would you excuse me?" Dee said. "Shelley, would you like a ride to your hotel?"

"Thanks. I'd like to visit with the girls for a little longer. I'll walk back to the bed-and-breakfast. And

Dee," she said in a strong Southern drawl, "thank you so much for arranging tonight. It means so much to me."

"You keep my card, and call if you need anything," Dee said, offering a hug. "Lauren, meet me at Seth's, okay?" Her sister nodded.

"Shelley, I'll drop you off at your hotel. We wouldn't recommend you go anywhere alone right now," Steff warned. "I think whoever killed Josie is still out there. All of these weird things started happening right after they found the skeleton. Someone thought their secrets were buried forever, and they aren't too happy that we're digging them all up, that's for sure."

TWENTY-TWO

"Dee." Edgar beckoned. "We need time to talk with the police before the press conference." He touched her shoulder, gently but firmly. "I'm sorry to push, but the president doesn't want to wait to make the announcement."

Dee looked at Edgar, fighting the temptation to collapse into his arms. She had never been so mentally weary in her life.

"Be careful getting home tonight, ladies." Edgar pulled out Dee's chair for her, and escorted her from the restaurant, wrapping his arm around her as if he sensed her exhaustion.

"Oh, wait, I need to pay the bill." Dee started to turn around and go back inside.

"I've already done that. Let's take my car so we can talk on the way. I'll bring you back to get yours later."

"Good thing, since I don't have a car. Still no rental." She looked at her watch and realized there wasn't time to argue. "Thank you. I'll pay you back."

"You don't need to worry about that." He paused. "What we need to worry about is finding the killer before anything else happens to anyone. I wasn't able to get through to you on your phone, so I took a chance that you hadn't changed your mind about where to take everyone. Had it not been for Cassie's red Mustang, I wouldn't have been sure you were in here."

She pulled her phone from her purse and saw four missed calls. "Oh, Edgar, I'm sorry, I didn't hear it ringing."

"Honestly, I'm happy it turned out this way. I'm glad you're not out alone tonight." Edgar's hand rested on the small of her back, a comforting gesture she could easily come to expect. "How'd it go?"

"It wasn't exactly fun, but it wasn't as maudlin as I thought it would be, either. We learned a lot."

"I'd certainly hope so, as long as it took." His half-smile confused her. Was he teasing?

"How long have you been waiting?" She glanced at the time on the calls and realized he'd started calling an hour and a half earlier.

"A while," Edgar said lightly. "I should have known better than to wait on a bunch of chatty women, shouldn't I?" One side of his mouth turned up. "So what did you find out?"

She looked at him and felt warm inside. In the past two weeks, he'd hardly uttered more than ten words to her that weren't work related, and yet he had sat outside a restaurant waiting for her.

"Dee?" he said softly. "Are you okay?"

"Oh, yeah," she said. "Just thinking how considerate you are, which doesn't *really* surprise me, but yet it does, sort of." *Especially this week.* "I used to think you were a bit chauvinistic. Now, I'm not so sure what to think."

"I don't know whether to be flattered, or put on warning." He paused, brushing his finger along her chin. "There'll be time to consider that later," he said as they reached his car. He offered his hand to help her keep her balance as she got inside the low sports car.

Dee glanced around outside, wondering when Magnolia Falls would return to the sedate Southern town that she loved. She longed to take leisurely walks, enjoy the warm evenings watching the stars. Before these crimes had been revealed, no one would have thought twice about walking around downtown at night.

Edgar started the car and took off toward the college.

"So the dental records were conclusive, huh?" Dee asked.

"Detective Anderson said they could take them to court, they're so perfect. Detective Anderson also said they just learned that evidence from our class archives has been destroyed by fire."

"Yeah, Shelley told us about that. Creepy, isn't it? That pretty well convinces me that someone was watching me that night." Edgar pulled up to the administration building and parked in the restricted spaces. The security guard met them at the car.

"They're meeting in the president's office tonight, Mr. Ortiz. Leave your car here. I'll make sure Parking doesn't give you a ticket," he joked.

Edgar forced a laugh. "Thanks, Randall."

Dee hurried on ahead to the president's office. There, they met the detectives, the president and J. T. Kessler.

Detective Anderson and the president of the college filled her in on the details to cover in the press conference. Dee asked a few questions while, out of the corner of her eye, she noticed J. T. Kessler pull Edgar aside. Edgar nodded, then shook his head and began talking with his hands, his frustration evident.

"Detective, have you looked at all into Penny Brighton? Several of us were visiting over dinner tonight. Shelley remembers Josie saying she was going to Europe after graduation with a pregnant friend, and Penny's name sounded familiar to Shelley. It seems she's the last person we've heard to have seen Josie." She glanced at her watch.

"She's been on our list for weeks since we found the charm. We haven't found anything on her, yet," the detective said.

"You might run that search under Kessler," J .T. Kessler said. "She married my son shortly before his death," he added. "I should have thought of that little tart immediately. Pardon me," he said.

"Excuse me, gentlemen," Dee said. "I'm going to go clear my head for a minute before the reporter is ready."

She noticed Edgar watching her every move, a grim smile plastered on his lips. Closing her eyes to focus and pray, Dee felt him step closer to her. "Is there anything I can do to help, Dee?"

She let out a deep sigh. "Pray."

"Already doing that."

"Then I guess we're covered, aren't we?"

Ten minutes later, Edgar listened as Dee spoke. He could hear the compassion in her voice. He could hear the love for Magnolia College and the determination to clean up its rapidly deteriorating reputation. "The police have identified the victim through a family contact and dental records. The name is being withheld until all family members have been contacted, but we can say she was a graduate of the class of 1998. The police now have narrowed the list of suspects to a few persons of interest and will share more information with the public in the coming days."

Edgar stood, frozen, admiring Dee's strength and courage as the reporters asked questions, hoping to trip her up and get the identity before anyone else.

Even when she'd been threatened and attacked, she'd put her fears aside to keep up with her responsibility. He kept his eyes on hers, offering the only support he could, prayer and presence. He wanted more than anything to tell Dee how much he cared for her, but as with everything in his life, his timing didn't seem to be the same as God's.

Lord, I know there are countless hurdles for us to

overcome, but I have no doubt they'll be worth jumping. I beg You to help me wait until the right time to tell Dee how I feel about her, and, I pray she's feeling the same for me.

After the cameras were put away, Edgar whisked Dee to his car. Once they were both in and had locked the doors, he paused to admire her. "You're holding up amazingly well."

She let out a deep sigh and leaned her head back against the seat. "If it keeps up much longer, I won't be. Seeing you there tonight helped me get through it."

"Good. I don't feel like I've done much to offer support recently, with so much traveling."

"It sounds like that's been worse than my job. I can't imagine how difficult it would be to accept students' rejections face-to-face. Magnolia College is such a good school. Which reminds me, Parker sent his endorsement today. It's very good."

"I'm glad you mentioned that," he said as they passed the college. "Do you mind if we just stop here and visit for a while?"

"That's fine. I have a feeling I'm not going to be happy about this, am I?"

He hesitated, evaluating her before he continued. "Probably not. I realized the other day that we've announced that the initials are P.B., so maybe it would be wise to wait a while before releasing his quote."

Dee didn't respond immediately, just stared at him. "You don't think Parker could do such a thing, do you?"

"Personally, me, no. I wouldn't have thought anyone in our class could have done anything so vile. But the fact remains that someone killed Josie Skerritt and left her body right here on campus. I wouldn't have imagined that Cornell Rutherford could have been involved in illegal gambling, either. Or that the coach is involved. My circle of trust is getting smaller each week." He pulled into a parking lot and stopped.

"Edgar," she groaned. "Why do you keep agreeing to something, then changing things? We set a strategy together. Why did you hire me if you don't want to let go of the way it's done?"

"This investigation is constantly changing our world, Dee, and we have to be one step ahead of what the public is thinking."

"We are, or were," she said, shaking her head. "But haven't they already cleared him? I mean, he's been around ever since the charm was found. He's not terribly sociable, I realize, but he wouldn't be walking around if he was seriously under suspicion, would he?"

"I don't know. Look at how short a time Coach Nelson was in jail. I'm actually surprised that Cornell isn't out yet, given his wife's wealth."

She scrunched up her face and dropped her forehead into her hands as Edgar brushed her hair off her face. "I'm sorry to make it so complicated, Dee."

"It's not you. I know you have a valid point with Parker, but…" Her voice faded away as she placed her hand over his. "I just wish it would be over. I'm tired of this roller coaster."

Edgar wanted to erase the worry from her delicate skin. "I understand, really."

"None of our lives are normal anymore. We are three blocks from the restaurant. We could have walked if it hadn't been for some killer still out there."

"Speaking of which, I suppose we're like sitting ducks here." Edgar started the car and pulled out onto the highway while they finished discussing the pros and cons of using Parker's endorsement.

"Maybe it would be better for Parker if we postponed it. Maybe he'd rather stay out of the limelight until they find the murderer. As a popular comic book writer, he doesn't need bad PR any more than the college does." Dee smiled slightly. "I hate it when you're right. I don't want to tell him now, though, after he's already agreed. Plus, he's lined up to go with us next week to recruit."

"You could point out that it would be to his benefit to stay low. Or if you'd prefer, I'd be happy to talk to him."

She rested her hand on the door handle. "Thanks for the offer, Edgar. I'll do it. You're going to be traveling again tomorrow, aren't you?"

He pulled into the space outside the restaurant. "Yes, but that only means I have time to burn. I'll call and talk to him tomorrow. Are you still staying at Seth's house?"

She shook her head. "No, Lauren and I are going

back home tonight since Rutherford was the one stalking us. With him in jail, we decided it's safe to go back."

He couldn't believe she would tell Josie's sister that the killer could still be out there, and not believe it pertained to herself. "Do you hear what you've said?"

"I'm not going home alone. Lauren is at Seth's waiting for me. And then we'll be together."

"What's wrong with staying at Seth's house until the murderer is found?" Edgar glanced around, making sure there wasn't still someone stalking her. "It's better safe than sorry. Besides, you look too tired to drive all the way out there."

As if he'd commanded it, she yawned. "I'll call Lauren and see if she can drive. I miss my own home." Dee looked around outside then pulled her cell phone from her purse and tried to reach Lauren. "So who is staying with Christiana while you're out so much?"

"She's been staying with family friends a lot these days. With the extra traveling I've been doing, I felt she needed the security that I had when I came to America. This week, she's staying with my host family."

"Because of the threat, and that picture of us outside my house?"

Edgar nodded. "I have to protect her. She's only seventeen, and if something happened to me, she'd be deported, sent back to my youngest brother in Brazil. I want someone caring for her who is familiar with what I've gone through."

"Oh, Edgar," she groaned. "I'm so sorry. I've made such a mess for you."

"I'm not worried about the picture. You know it was nothing. I know it, your sister can verify it, and so would Steff. Don't worry, Dee. I'm really only concerned about Christiana staying here. Hopefully, they could pull some strings to keep her here until our resident alien cards are approved. I've been very blessed with good friends who have opened their arms to Christiana and me." Edgar paused and looked at the vehicles in the parking lot. "Where did you park?"

Dee pointed to a space a few cars away. "I'm calling Lauren to be sure she took it." When Lauren didn't answer, Dee opened her phone again. "Seth, it's Dee. Lauren didn't answer her cell, isn't she there with you?" Dee looked around and shrugged. "I'll call you back." She ended the call and again dialed her sister.

Edgar looked around, surprised that there were so many cars around the restaurant. "Do you think they're still inside?"

"Seth said he called the restaurant an hour ago and they said the party had left before the news." Dee clapped her hands to her face. "Please, God, let me find them safe and sound."

"None of these cars are theirs?" Edgar asked. "Isn't that Lauren's station wagon?"

"No, hers is blue."

"And Cassie's red Mustang isn't here. What do the others drive?"

Dee looked around, panic hitting her again.

"They're not here. Edgar," she said, shaking, "don't leave me alone, please."

TWENTY-THREE

"It's okay. I'm not going anywhere without you," he insisted, taking her into his embrace. His strong arms around her felt like a shield of armor protecting her.

"I don't know what I'd do without you, Edgar. Not through all of this. What if something has happened to them?" Dee felt her heart beating faster.

"There were what, five or six of you at dinner? They have to be fine. Did you talk about going anywhere else?"

Dee shook her head.

"Do you have any of the others' phone numbers? Let's try calling them."

Dee pulled out her cell phone and dialed Steff, but she was forced to leave her a message. "Let's get back in the car. Would you take me to the bed-and-breakfast on Peach Tree Lane? Maybe they went together to drop Shelley off and decided to stay for a while."

None of the cars were outside the bed-and-break-fast, but Dee ran inside to see if Shelley had returned yet.

She waited at the desk as the night clerk took her time getting to the desk. "Hello, I had dinner with Shelley Johnson earlier, and had to leave the restaurant before she was ready to go. I can't reach any of the other women and want to make sure they're okay."

"I'm sorry, Miss Owens. That violates our policies."

"Yes, I understand. Could you ring her room for me then? I'm looking for my sister and friends, and need to know if they're okay."

The clerk was hesitant. "It's nearly eleven at night, ma'am."

"I just need to make sure they're okay. With all of the weird things going on in town lately, surely you realize we have to watch out for each other, don't you?"

"One try," the college-age girl said nervously. "But if the guest gets upset, I'm going to have my supervisor call you."

"That's fine. I'm sure Shelley won't be mad at you."

She hit the room number and waited. "Hello, Ms. Johnson. Miss…"

"Dee Owens."

"Okay, I'll send her up." She hung up and gave Dee the room number. "Up the stairs on the left."

Dee ran upstairs, to be met by Shelley. "Hi, Shelley, I'm sorry to bother you. I've been trying to find Lauren, and she's not back at her fiancé's house yet. Do you know where they went?"

"We went by a coffee place that has to-die-for cobbler and to watch the news. You handled the press very nicely. Mom and Dad said to thank you for respecting our privacy. They're coming up tomorrow with my husband and kids."

"It's going to be difficult for them, I'm sure."

Shelley nodded. "They're feeling so guilty. All these years they were sure she'd just run off. And they blamed themselves. Would you like to come in?"

"No thank you. Edgar's waiting outside for me." And she couldn't wait to get back to see him. "I didn't know where else to try. I'm sorry to have bothered you." The stress was starting to get the best of her. "If there is anything we can do, let me know, please."

"Thank you. We want desperately to find her little girl. And if we can find anyone who knows who the father may be, to make contact with him, too."

Dee felt the tears brewing. "I hope we can bring you all together." She backed toward the stairs, anxious to get back to Edgar's car to call Seth's house again. "Good night."

"Be careful Dee, and God bless."

Dee hurried through the exit and ran right into Edgar. "Shelley is upstairs, but the others…"

"Your sister just called. She's fine and just arrived at Seth's. And Steff called, she's home fine," he held up her phone.

"Thank you," she said softly. "You know, I was totally, totally, wrong..."

"Shh. We've both been wrong, Dee. Let's not focus on anything else right now. Let's keep thinking of the good things that God wants for us. Hold on to that hope. One day soon, this will all be behind us."

A few minutes later, Edgar walked Dee into Seth's house, still trying to convince her it was too late to drive out to her house. "Seth, Lauren, help me convince her to stay here tonight."

"Edgar's right, Dee. It's late, and you've just made another announcement. On the chance that it isn't Cornell stalking you, I think it's best to hang out here for a day or two more," her sister said.

"Fine," Dee consented, brushing her hair off her forehead with her hand. "Edgar, would you stay for some coffee?"

He smiled, remembering their last late-night coffee. "One cup, if it's not too much work."

"Not at all. I can even manage without the chef's assistance."

"Good, because I have an early delivery tomorrow. I'm going to bed. Night, y'all," Lauren said. "There are pecan pie bars in the cake server if you'd like a bite of dessert."

Dee raised her eyebrows. "Hmm, that might even call for a second cup of coffee."

"Dee, you know how to reset the security alarm, right?"

She nodded. "Thanks, Seth, I'll take care of it when Edgar leaves."

"G'night all."

Edgar said good-night, feeling like a teenager again. "Are you sure you want to offer coffee, Dee? I know you're..."

"Edgar, if you don't want to stay, I won't keep you," she said, giving him a chance to run. "But I think it's time we sorted a few things out, and there doesn't seem to be a better time."

"I'll stay," he said as he took a step closer. "I called Christiana from the press conference and told her that I thought she'd be safest staying with Reverend Roger's family tonight, so I've nowhere I'd rather be."

Dee's tired, ashen face regained color. "And there's no cat to attack you."

"I'd even face Tipsy if it meant being with you." Edgar held out his hand. "So what is it you want to talk about this time?"

"Us. You, me, our jobs. My faith. I'm not picky, where'd you like to start." She turned and walked into the kitchen and pulled the coffeemaker from the cabinet. "Well?"

"That's quite a list."

"It's been a long month of not being able to share with each other, Edgar. Was I imagining things? Weren't we getting close?"

"Of course we were," he said, taking a step toward her. "Dee, this has killed me too. I don't know how to reassure you right now. I don't want to leave another hole if this case doesn't end soon."

She studied him closely. "What was J. T. Kessler talking to you about tonight?"

"It's premature to discuss that." Why had J.T. told him they were going to ask Dee to take this job full-time? he asked himself. Didn't he see the struggle this was for him and Dee? Hadn't he heard the rumors? She'd never get the respect that she deserved here.

He could see the disappointment in her face. It was killing her not to know something. He wanted so desperately to hold her and kiss her and leave the problems behind them, but that wasn't who either of them was. "Trust me, Dee. Please. It's not that I want to keep a secret from you. It's something that's totally out of my hands."

"Is it about your job?"

"No, it's not, but because I'm sure your next question is going to be what the provost had to tell me—the board has decided to cancel the search for director of admissions and leave me as interim."

Her lips twitched. "One foot in the door isn't always a comfortable position to be in, is it?"

He shook his head. "There are benefits, for me as well as the college, and I'm trying to stay focused on those for now."

"Such as?"

"First of all, it gives us time to figure out if we're headed in the same direction. It gives me a chance to really decide if this is where God wants me."

"Or if you want to stay at Magnolia College…you are part of that decision, remember?"

He smiled. "For a minute, you reminded me of my mother. And that's a compliment."

Dee blushed. "I wish I'd had a chance to have met her. I'm sure I'd have loved her, since she raised you."

"Careful," he said.

The coffeepot gurgled that the end of the pot had brewed and Dee turned to get cups. "Would you like a pecan bar with your coffee?"

"Sure." He looked at her back and the droop of her shoulders. He stepped to her side and rested his hand on her shoulder. "Dee, I've never cared for a woman as deeply as I do for you. And had it not been for this skeleton, I would have taken that leap after the reunion. Haven't I explained that?"

"Yes, you have, Edgar, but it seems like things changed after Detective Anderson questioned us about Josie and Penny." She hesitated, as if expecting him to remember something. She turned around and leaned against the counter. "When we talked about my faith, and my social life?"

"My mind wasn't even there. Things have been difficult to say the best. I don't remember what I said, but if I said something that hurt you, I'm sorry, Dee. Truly, I am. I hate that I asked you to take this job, and I'm incredibly apologetic that I've been so difficult to work with."

Dee's cell phone rang, startling both of them. "That ring is my security alarm. Something happened at the house," she said, grabbing her purse.

"Let the police handle it, Dee."

"Oh, they'll respond, but I need to meet them there." She ran to the door. "I'll take Lauren's car, Edgar. Go on home."

He took hold of her hand and pulled her into his arms. "Don't go, please. You can't do anything now. This is why you came here, to be out of danger."

"I can't sit back and do nothing—that's not who I am."

"You installed a security system to let someone else do something. The police don't need you there. Whatever is done is done." He gazed into her eyes, losing his heart more each moment. "Please."

Dee closed her eyes, rested her head on his shoulder and whispered, "God, help me learn to let go of my need to control things around me. Help me learn to hand my problems to you, and not keep yanking them back. And thank you for my friends, who have been here with me through all of this."

"Obrigado, Nosso Senhor."

Dee raised her head and looked into his eyes. *"Obriagado Noso Señhor?* What does that mean?"

"Thank You, Lord. *Obrigado* is 'thank you,' *Nosso Senhor* is 'our Lord.' There's no extra *a* in *obrigado.*"

She watched his lips as he said it and smiled. "And what are you thanking Him for?"

"You asking God back into your life."

"He was never really gone. Just guiding me when I was too stubborn to recognize it." She raised her hand to his jaw and touched it lightly. "In my heart, I know He's been here, protecting me, placing his shield of armor around me."

Edgar smiled. "That's wonderful, Dee. I didn't question it, but I'm glad that you trust me with what's in your heart." It felt right to have her in his arms.

Her phone rang again, and Dee answered. The caller's voice was loud enough that he could hear it. "Dee, this is the security center. The police have investigated your alarm, and found no problems outside. They did see a cat inside batting at the windows. Maybe that set the alarm off, if he hit it hard enough."

Edgar laughed.

So did Dee. "That would be Tipsy. Thank you for the call." She closed the phone and gazed up to him. "I don't think that was a coincidence, do you?"

He shook his head.

"*Eu te amo* means I love you."

She got a goofy grin on her lips, luscious-looking lips that he wanted to kiss—again and again. "I think I'm going to like learning a new language. *Eu te amo*. Do you mean it, or are you just teaching me another phrase?"

"I thought you might want to know what's in my heart."

Her face glowed. "I do. I like knowing secrets you know." She raised her eyebrows. "No, I love knowing secrets, especially that one. And as long as we need to keep it quiet, that's fine by me. I just needed to know."

Edgar laughed. "Let's hope we don't have to keep it a secret for long." He kissed her tenderly, then stepped away. "I think you'd better get to sleep, and I need to get home. I have an early morning tomorrow."

TWENTY-FOUR

A few days later, Dee logged on to the Web site, searching for any sign of the new settings before they got the site up and running again. She wasn't a hacker, but she couldn't see any difference.

Steff had consulted with her family's lawyer, who agreed that the messages about Cornell hadn't been damaging yet, but it was still wise to have the police monitor messages before they went out to the public to avoid any future problems. Therefore, it was a lot more time-consuming than it had been. The good thing was, the police were still doing most of it.

Dee opened her e-mail each day, more and more anxious to hear from Edgar. Though he could still annoy her more than any man had in years, he was trying to make her feel special and appreciated even when he disagreed with her. She spent Tuesday and Wednesday catching up with her clients in Savannah, thankful for a break from Magnolia Falls.

Edgar e-mailed the details of the Charleston re-cruiting fair the next week, and Dee finalized the necessary arrangements. They would have three schools to stop at, and the schedule would be full. As he met with prospective students who had applied before the scandals hit the news, it had become apparent that they were delaying committing to attend in the fall. Edgar was getting increasingly worried. She could tell from his e-mails that he was losing hope.

Thursday afternoon, as she was getting ready to leave the office, an unexpected visitor showed up in the doorway of her office. She started to tell her assistant not to send anyone back to her office, then realized it was too late.

"I asked your assistant to let me announce myself," Edgar said with a grin. "I hope you don't mind."

Dee felt her heart sending her entire blood supply to her face. "Mind? No." When had a flirtatious man made her blush? When had she cared about anyone this much? "How was your trip?"

He shook his head. "We'll have time to talk about that tomorrow, if you'll be in the office."

It must not have gone well, she thought. "I plan on it." She wasn't sure she was going to want to push him to talk about it right away. He looked worn-out.

"Christiana is helping Cassie with the career-shadowing program meeting tonight, so I hoped I could steal you away for a while," he said with a smile. "Do you have plans for dinner?"

"You mean it's okay while we're out of sight of the college?"

"I don't want you hurt..." His voice trailed off and he shrugged.

She waited for him to finish. And waited. Finally she had to ask. "And how do you think people knowing we're seeing each other outside the office is going to hurt me?"

He closed her office door and sat down in the chair across from her. "I try to keep my home life away from the office, which is very difficult in an office full of women."

"So that's your strategy. I knew you had to be part saint to deal with a dozen female coworkers," she teased. "Just to be sure I'm clear here, what do they tease you about?"

"When I was hired, they seemed to think all Brazilian men are playboys. Finally they figured out I am about as far from that as can be. Then they decided I was okay, I guess, because everyone had a friend or relative that they wanted to set me up with. Everyone was determined to marry me off. But I don't want my coworkers involved in my personal life."

"So are you here to fire me?" Dee raised an eyebrow.

Edgar laughed, deep and heartily. "Not a chance. I'm here to apologize for the other evening, for telling you to ignore your home. I was very concerned for you and I'm afraid that my protective nature sometimes takes control. I realized how insensitive I was."

She thought through her next words carefully. "Thank you for the apology, but I have to admit, it felt good to let someone else say it's okay to step away." She glanced at him, stunned by the sparkle in his dark brown eyes. "I realize it's not a good idea to get involved with a coworker, Edgar, but Magnolia College is not my primary employer, nor will it be. J.T. offered me the job. Is that what he told you at the press conference last week?"

"Yes, but it wasn't my place to tell you. Why are you turning it down?"

"I like diversity. I don't want to put all of my eggs in one basket. Plus, I'm hoping to avoid any conflict of interest. This assignment is only temporary and it will stay temporary."

"You don't have to sell me. After being away from you this week I've realized I don't want to miss this chance to see if we might be right for each other. But I don't want to stand in the way of your career, Dee."

"I love my career and I love Magnolia College, but not nearly as much as I love you, Edgar. My faith and my family come first, I've learned that through all of this. God hasn't let me down, and I'm not going to let Him down again. And if you want the director's job, I'll do everything I can to help you get it. I hope you've not backed away because of me, thinking I wanted the marketing position?"

"I convinced myself that it would be okay either way. Sometimes I get so comfortable where I'm at that I don't want to push to the next level."

She admired him, his honesty, his ethical standards. "I'd be happy to offer a few suggestions to get the director's job if you want to try pushing a little."

"I believe that the last five years' experience here will speak louder than any half-court shot as the buzzer rings. Through all of this, I've learned that who I'm with through life means far more than where I'm at, or what I'm doing. If they want to wait five more months to make a decision, that gives you and me time to finalize God's plans for us."

"You mean, go public…"

"I mean, I'd like everyone to know that I've fallen in love with you, Dee. That I hope to spend the rest of my life with you." He pulled a small box from his coat pocket. "I was going to do this over a candlelight dinner."

Tears shimmered in Dee's beautiful blue eyes, and Edgar could see the ocean in them. She covered her mouth with her hands. "Oh."

"Oh?"

"Ahh. I don't know what to say." She fanned herself. "I mean, I wasn't expecting this. Not so soon. I mean, I wanted…I hoped…"

He laughed. "It's rather frightening to see Dee Owens speechless." He opened the box and showed her the ring, then got down on one knee. "Deandra Owens, would you give me the honor of becoming my wife?"

"It would be my honor, Edgar. The ring is beautiful."

"Not nearly as beautiful as the woman wearing it," he said as he pushed it onto her finger. He kissed it, sealing it in place. *"Eu te amo, amado meu."*

"Oh, me too. What you said," she whispered. "I'm all tongue-tied. I don't want to say it wrong and make a mess of a perfect proposal."

"If it's not micromanaging too much, might I

suggest we have the ceremony soon, in case I get the position. I wouldn't want to ignore my beautiful bride."

"And maybe you could take me to meet your family in Brazil? I've always wanted to go there. Are the beaches as beautiful as I've heard?"

"Almost as beautiful as you," he said with another kiss. "I can't think of a better vacation. Christiana could go along and stay with family while we honeymoon."

Dee pulled out her calendar. "I have two weeks in May that are pretty light. How does that sound?"

"It sounds like a long way off, but we can keep negotiating over dinner. I'd like you to come with me to tell Christiana after dinner, if that doesn't make it too late."

"I hope she'll be as happy to have a sister as I am to have another one. I should call Lauren, let her know I'll not be home for dinner. Or…maybe we should pick up Christiana and take her to Seth's so we can tell them all together." Dee gathered her purse and stood to leave, then turned to grab her electronic day planner. "Oh my, it's hard to believe how quickly life changes."

"It's never been a nicer change at a more perfect time. When I think how many years it took for God to bring us together I'm so grateful. We've been in His sights all along as He has been preparing us for each other."

* * * * *

*In May 2008, some of Magnolia Falls's
mysteries will be solved. Don't miss
A FACE IN THE SHADOWS by Lenora Worth,
the fifth installment in*
REUNION REVELATIONS.

Dear Reader,

Dee and Edgar were a real challenge for me, but by the time I was done writing *In His Sights*, I loved them more than I think I have any of my other characters. They had real struggles working to tear them apart. Struggles I could relate to, anyway. No, I don't have murderers chasing me down, but I have had my share of hurdles in life these last few years.

Sometimes it seems the harder I strive to do the right thing—to make things better—they only get worse. It's very difficult for me personally to accept that God isn't only answering my prayers, but He's also working to make someone else's life turn out the way He planned. And sometimes that means one of our prayers isn't going to turn out the way we wanted. I'm only one little part of God's plan.

My greatest struggle is to look at the bright side. Finding blessings that come out of a terrible situation has become a goal of mine. God has many of them hidden in my world, and I've found it's a very healing way to approach life. I don't have to be in control, making sure everything turns out perfectly, I just need to turn it over to God and let Him work through me to do my part.

I hope that you find the bright spots shining in the shadows of life, just like Edgar and Dee were able to find their love for each other in the midst of a crisis. If you have time to write, I'd love to hear from you about the blessings you've found in the shadows. You can write me at <u>csteward37@aol.com</u> or P.O. Box 200286, Evans, Co 80620.

God Bless,

Carol Steward

QUESTIONS FOR DISCUSSION

1. Dee has silently struggled with her faith for years. What made her question her faith? Have you ever questioned your faith? How did you work through your questions?

2. Edgar's faith has been strong and visible, causing Dee to doubt herself even more. It's important for us to realize that God has a different plan and purpose for each of us and we should not compare ourselves to others. Have you ever looked at yourself and compared your faith to that of someone else? Practice looking for the positive things about your life that God wants you to put to good use. What do you think those things might be? How do you think God wants you to use those gifts?

3. Edgar struggles with his feelings about Dee because he questions her faith based upon her past. How did he handle his questions? Was that the right way to deal with them? What could he have done differently?

4. Office romances create many challenges. How do you think coworkers should deal with the attraction?

5. Dee believes that Annie's family used their faith as a crutch. Is there such thing as using God as a crutch? How can we avoid this misconception?

6. Is love truly blind? What does this statement mean?

7. Sometimes Dee had to go against what Edgar wanted for the publicity in order to help the police solve the cases at hand. What do you do when your job or boss requires you to do or act against your beliefs? How does God instruct us to follow our leaders?

8. Dee has very strong beliefs about ignoring the gifts that God has given us. What gifts has God given you? How does God use those gifts through you? How else might God want you to use your talents?

9. Dee found it very difficult to let others help her, protect her, love her. She's always called the shots. How did God break down the walls Dee built around herself? Has God helped you to break down walls around you? How did you feel? How did you overcome those feelings?

10. Beauty is a real contention for Dee. Why do you think it bothered her to be noticed for her appearance? Is that wrong of her? Why do you think that when Edgar told her she was beautiful, she was able to accept his compliment instead of becoming defensive?

11. Edgar also has a difficult time letting go of his control, especially when it comes to his career. He knows that what is best for the individuals could end up costing him his job. How does he

finally overcome his struggle? Have you ever had a time when you know doing the "right" thing is going to hurt, maybe even cost you something you cherish? How did you come to a decision on handling the issue?

12. Dee realizes that God has brought Edgar into her life and at the same time brought balance to her life, her emotions and her expectations, personally and professionally. Is that realistic? How do the people God brings into your life complement you? Do you ever look at those relationships and think what your life would be like without them? Do you ask God to be with you in your work and personal friendships as well as romantic relationships? How could that change your job? Your life? Your outlook?

REQUEST YOUR FREE BOOKS!
2 FREE RIVETING INSPIRATIONAL NOVELS
PLUS 2 FREE MYSTERY GIFTS

YES! Please send me 2 FREE Love Inspired® Suspense novels and my 2 FREE mystery gifts (gifts are worth about $10). After receiving them, if I don't wish to receive any more books, I can return the shipping statement marked "cancel". If I don't cancel, I will receive 4 brand-new novels every month and be billed just $4.24 per book in the U.S. or $4.74 per book in Canada, plus 25¢ shipping and handling per book and applicable taxes, if any*. That's a savings of over 20% off the cover price! I understand that accepting the 2 free books and gifts places me under no obligation to buy anything. I can always return a shipment and cancel at any time. Even if I never buy another book, the two free books and gifts are mine to keep forever.

123 IDN ERXX 323 IDN ERXM

Name	(PLEASE PRINT)	
Address		Apt. #
City	State/Prov.	Zip/Postal Code

Signature (if under 18, a parent or guardian must sign)

Order online at www.LoveInspiredSuspense.com
Or mail to Steeple Hill Reader Service:
IN U.S.A.: P.O. Box 1867, Buffalo, NY 14240-1867
IN CANADA: P.O. Box 609, Fort Erie, Ontario L2A 5X3

Not valid to current subscribers of Love Inspired Suspense books.

Want to try two free books from another series?
Call 1-800-873-8635 or visit www.morefreebooks.com

* Terms and prices subject to change without notice. N.Y. residents add applicable sales tax. Canadian residents will be charged applicable provincial taxes and GST. This offer is limited to one order per household. All orders subject to approval. Credit or debit balances in a customer's account(s) may be offset by any other outstanding balance owed by or to the customer. Please allow 4 to 6 weeks for delivery. Offer available while quantities last.

Your Privacy: Steeple Hill Books is committed to protecting your privacy. Our Privacy Policy is available online at www.SteepleHill.com or upon request from the Reader Service. From time to time we make our lists of customers available to reputable third parties who may have a product or service of interest to you. If you would prefer we not share your name and address, please check here. ☐

LISUS08

Love Inspired SUSPENSE

TITLES AVAILABLE NEXT MONTH

Don't miss these four stories in May

DANGER IN A SMALL TOWN by Ginny Aiken
Carolina Justice

Former DEA agent Ethan Rogers is done investigating crimes...until Tess Graver moves into the neighborhood. A sinister force has followed her. Though Ethan tries to stay distant, he's drawn to protect her.

A FACE IN THE SHADOWS by Lenora Worth
Reunion Revelations

The promising friendship between Kate Brooks and Parker Buchanan is threatened when the police begin questioning him about a decade-old murder. Kate believes that Parker is innocent, but her faith may cost her. The real killer is setting them up for a double murder: their own.

BAYOU JUDGMENT by Robin Caroll

Felicia Trahan is overjoyed with her new lease on life. She loves the freedom of working with Pastor Spencer Bertrand and rooming with her friend, Jolie. Then Jolie turns up murdered. Dealing with threats, attacks and Spencer's dark past will take all Felicia's strength—and faith.

DEADLY EXPOSURE by Cara Putman

A night at the theater turns deadly when reporter Dani Richards stumbles into a murder scene. With the killer on her tail, Dani discovers that her ex-boyfriend Caleb Jamison is the only one who can keep her safe.

LISCNM0408